WANDER
LOVE

WANDER
LOVE

rachel
blaufeld

This one is for my beagles—Cadillac and Cruise.
Yep, that's right. By my side, day or night, snoring and supporting.
They don't know how to make coffee or proofread, but
they sure know how to make a gal feel loved.

And for Cassius, my big, beautiful, gentle, kind Lab, who crossed over the
Rainbow Bridge a few moons ago. I miss you, good buddy.
This book's got a Labrador just for you.

ABOUT THE BOOK

Sick of living under her dad's rules, Emerson Bender bolts when she's eighteen. On her own for the first time, she heads to the only place her mom ever lived—New York City—desperate to find the woman who dropped her off on her dad's doorstep.

Content to spend the rest of his life in Small Town, Pennsylvania, Price Barnes is plucked out of his idyllic life by his estranged father. Missing his mom and stepfather, he's dropped in New York City to attend college and live an all-expenses-paid lifestyle. Cushy, right? But not the life he wanted.

She's looking to fill a hole in her heart, and he's looking to forget the man who disrupted his life. Together, they're both wandering, looking for acceptance and hoping to forget the rejection.

CHAPTER
ONE

Emerson

"**E**merson! Stop. Don't do this! Emerson, please don't do this. I didn't mean it. Please, Emmy . . ."

His words echoed in my head but didn't stop me. I slammed the car door right in my dad's face, shutting him up in mid-plea.

I couldn't listen to him.

Didn't dare.

Not for one second longer.

Not this time.

Not even when he called me *Emmy*.

We'd had this fight before—a million and two times. Each time, I gave in and did it his way. Our fights always ended with me crying on his shoulder, and him rubbing my back, shushing me and telling me to let it go.

Just the thought of it made me grit my teeth.

The last time, I'd sworn to never bring *her* up again, and he'd said the same. It was a mutual decision. Yet, I was the one to break our promise. I was the one who dared speak her name aloud.

Five stupid letters, P-A-U-L-A, came tumbling from my lips, inside the four walls of our house, the exact place where I'd promised not to say it.

Paula had always been and continued to be a curse word between us—worse than *fuck*. Her name was only brought out when the big guns were needed, or when the most painful wound needed to be inflicted. The mere mention of her name left a gaping gash in us that no superglue or stitches would easily remedy.

Which is why he'd spent my whole life convincing me she needed to stay where she'd always been—deep in my past.

Although I tried not to bring her up in regular conversation, Paula haunted my dreams and waking hours in equal measure. Dad was the better person, and only spoke of her when I was bold enough to say her name first.

Except this time, I wasn't full of piss and vinegar and false threats.

Boldly, I'd said her name loud and proud. For once in my short life, I took him to task. I was determined to find her, and he wasn't going to stop me. He was squeezing the life out of me with his rules and curfews.

Yeah, I was all he had, and he'd been a single dad since I was born, but *fuck it*. The man had been my rock, but he was also a major pain in my ass.

Like right now, waving his hands in the air, begging me to stop.

Not gonna do it, Dad.

This time, he'd gone too far. He had no right to tell me I couldn't date Robby Williams. Actually, dating I could do. It was the other stuff Dad wouldn't allow.

So what if I wanted to stay out with Robby . . . all night? I was eighteen, had just graduated from high school, and would be off to school in the fall. I could do whatever I wanted, even if I still lived at home. Right?

"Paula would let me do it." Tired of always giving in, this time I'd held my ground, threatening him with the only thing I knew would hurt. It wouldn't just sting; it would bite like a samurai sword slicing through raw flesh. Any other threat would have cut like a butter knife.

He stared at me, taking in my angry face and heaving chest before boldly daring me. "Fine, Emerson, be my guest. Go find your long-lost mommy and see if she cares."

As soon as he'd said it, he broke down and cupped my cheeks, his calloused palms gentle on my skin. "I didn't mean it, honey, I swear. This is hard. I can't always be the perfect mom and dad, all at the same time."

With what I was certain had to be a thousand red splotches creeping up my neck, I decided to go for it. Take him up on his challenge and go look for Paula. After all, in three short months, I'd be gone anyway. *What's wrong with setting out a little early?*

Somehow, I reversed out of the driveway without hitting anything and threw the car in drive, watching with one eye as my dad's silhouette disappeared in the rearview mirror.

With the windows down, my long hair blowing behind me, I cranked up the radio. It didn't escape me that I didn't have a clue where I was going or who I was even looking for, but that was me. Impulsive, determined, misguided—a dangerous combination—but me, nonetheless.

With a few thousand dollars saved up from working every weekend, and a nice savings bond left me in my grandpap's will, I decided I was actually doing it. I was going to find my mom and bring her back.

Period.

At the very least, I was going to ask her why she left.

"I'm eighteen," I mumbled to myself as I drove on. "Anyway, what does he know about being a woman . . . a grown woman? Plus, I'm perfectly capable of driving. Legally, I am a grown woman, right?"

A long, drawn-out string of nonsensical words spun from my mouth as I drove on, even though no one sat in the passenger seat to hear them. But it didn't seem to bother me.

I was on my own for the first time in my life, and it felt good. Exciting. Freeing.

When I got my driver's license at sixteen, my dad had been by my side, but there was no party or fun dinner at a restaurant to celebrate. Although, he did buy me a used Toyota to overcompensate for his blundering through my first period and puberty.

It had been just my dad and me for my whole life, so I didn't really know he was blundering anything until much later, when my friends and I got to talking. I guess I could have gone to one of their moms with my questions, but to be honest, most of my friends were boys.

"Platonic, of course," I mumbled to myself.

It was no shock that most of my friends were boys. After all, I was raised by a single dad and grew up speaking "male." That didn't mean I wasn't desperate for a woman's touch, soft murmurings from a mom I never knew, secret chats and pillow talk—some semblance of what I'd seen portrayed on TV and in the movies.

The thing was, my reality was a far cry from the movies. My mom, Paula Dubois, was a real class act—in her own mind. She'd come from some hoity-toity, rich-ass, snobby family, according to my grandpap. She'd never had a hard day in her life except when she went slumming with my dad, and subsequently, nine months later. Also my grandpap's words.

I stole a quick glance at my jet-black hair in the rearview mirror—compliments of Paula, I was told. My dad was all blond hair and blue eyes. Too bad his recessive genes didn't duke it out hard enough. My coloring was a constant reminder of Paula for him with my dark hair and green eyes. Except when it came to my facial features . . . then I was a female version of him.

When my parents met, my dad was no more than the son of a seaside construction worker. Paula had been vacationing near the beach town where he'd lived his whole life. Sea Isle City, New Jersey, was all my dad had known.

The story went something like this . . .

Paula went to Atlantic City for a bachelorette weekend. She'd been sitting in the bar, sipping on a glass of bubbly, when my dad and some buddies made their way into the lounge. They were already half-drunk on cheap beer and high on playing poker when they bellied up to the bar. According to my dad, Billy Bender—or Bend, as his friends liked to call him—my mom eyed him up immediately. He ditched his friends that night, warming the sheets of Paula's luxury hotel bed. The next morning, she rode back to Sea Isle with him and spent a month shacked up in his run-down beach bungalow.

She'd been twenty-one and he'd been twenty-five. Paula was on the brink of everything. My dad had close to nothing on the horizon, *"Other than a ready woman and an ice-cold beer at the end of the day,"* according to my dad.

My mom sunbathed, applying a healthy dose of expensive-as-shit oils on her silky skin—at least that's what I'd always envisioned—while Bend worked. When he got home at the end of the day, they went at it like rabbits, drinking wine on the back deck, and then stronger coffee in the morning. The latter I also knew, compliments of Pap.

"Hey, I'm eighteen. I know where babies come from. That's how I came to be—the going-at-it-like-rabbits part."

Embarrassed at talking to myself again, I turned up the radio. Lush green trees and large fields of crops I couldn't name blurred past the car windows as I sped down the highway. Yet, nothing could distract me from the story in my head . . .

When the month was up, Paula was already bored and went back to her uppity college in New York City. Apparently, my grandpap had predicted this.

Abandoned, my lonely dad hunkered down for the fall and winter in his little beach town, picking up the odd construction job and rehabbing houses, and forgot about the fiery city girl who had warmed his bed.

Then, come spring, Paula showed up one afternoon with a snarky, sure-of-herself friend on her left and a baby carrier on her right.

That would have been me.

She'd said, "Here. You left me with a little souvenir of Sea Isle. I wasn't so fond of this place to begin with . . . so, here it is."

It! Not *her*. Not *she*. No name, nothing. All per my grandpap. My dad tried to sugarcoat the story, but there wasn't much to work with.

With my mom standing on the porch, baby in tow, my dad apparently went mute. He tried to form words, but he couldn't.

"I just couldn't stop staring at you. The most precious baby girl I'd ever seen."

I'd finally pulled the truth out of him when I was around twelve or thirteen with constant prodding for more information.

Like his dad, he embellished. *"I suppose it's because you were so beautiful, sitting there in your carrier, all pretty in purple."*

I'd tried to tell him over and over again . . . "Dad, the expression is pink. Pretty in pink, not purple."

But he always insisted that's why he'd gone mute. My prettiness.

I'd believed him until I was around sixteen.

Anyway, my mom had added insult to my dad's bruised ego, saying, "By the time I figured out what the hell was wrong with my body, it was too late to do anything about it. I thought it was all the cheap beer making me fat, but it wasn't. It was this girl. So, she's all yours."

She sat my carrier down on the porch with a white patent leather diaper bag (he still had it when I was a teen) and turned to leave, her friend never saying a word.

"What's her name?" my dad had called after them.

"Whatever the hell you want," Paula had said over her shoulder as she left.

I'd been five days old, according to my birth certificate.

My dad said his life changed forever that day. He'd loved me the instant he set eyes on me, and he didn't regret a moment of raising me himself.

Other than when I was desperate to spend the night with Robby. After all, a girl couldn't go off to college without her V-card punched. I deserved a night or two with my high school love.

My poor dad. I was a pain in the ass, always looking for a little mischief, and he never was able to have any fun or fuck like rabbits anymore.

But at least he kept me.

Oh, and about my name. I was named Emerson, after my grandfather, who used to bounce me on his knee and hide eggs at Easter for me.

My dad will never admit it, but the *P* in my middle name, Paige, was meant for my mom, who he seemed to want to honor in some way.

"She gave me you, Emerson," he always used to tell me.

And in turn, I gave you grief, Dad.

CHAPTER
TWO

Price

I didn't care what anyone else said . . . New York City was a shithole. It was almost as if the air hung heavy with wasted money and expensive booze. I could barely breathe there.

Give me Main Street, USA, over this cranky city, any day of the week, and I'd be good to go.

My feet pounded the sidewalk for a run at dawn, the dirty, murky, disease-infested water rushing down the gutter splashing my ankles. People said they loved this place, but I didn't believe them.

It wasn't even light out yet, and this place was so fucking noisy and busy. Horns and ambulances blared all around me. Clubbers and drag queens walked home, laughing in the twilight.

Welcome to the Big Rotten Apple.

After I'd lapped the entirety of Central Park, savoring the briefest moments of quiet on the back side, I made my way home. To my apartment in the looming building on Central Park South. *Yep, you heard me right.*

I'd recently come into some money.

In fact, I was like a pig in shit, practically rolling in it.

Problem was, the money had strings, and I didn't like them all too much. I'd rather be covered in hay and dirt, wearing ripped jeans, my hair too long, my nose sunburned and my hands blistered from a hard day's work outside.

"Morning, Rudy," I said to the doorman as I wiped my feet on the entryway carpet. I wasn't raised in a barn—it had been a nice-size farmhouse—and I knew better than to track my wet feet all over the lobby.

"Good morning, Mr. Barnes. Ready for the weekend?"

Poor guy, he startled hard when I slapped my hand on the counter in front of him.

"Cut it out, Rudy. It's Price. Barnes is *his* last name. Price is all me, only me, even if I do share his last name."

"Yes, sir. I mean, Mr. Price. Did you have a good run?"

"Price. Just Price. Didn't get far enough, only chased a few demons this morning. Too many left to slay for a lonely day in the big city."

Rudy probably knew me better than anyone here. I hadn't made many friends since I'd been brought to this godforsaken urban mecca a month ago. Sometimes, I carried a beer down and sat with Rudy, rambling about how much I missed home. He was there the day I arrived with shitkickers on my feet, nothing but a T-shirt and a flannel on my back, my dark hair wild and unruly—like my heart.

I couldn't help the smug smirk on my face. How a good ole boy from Central Pennsylvania ended up in this sea of vapidness was as big a mystery to me as it was to him. One minute I'd been sitting on top of the water tower, looking out at the fields in front of me, and the next, I'd been in the back of a shiny black town car, on my way to New York City.

I was making the most of it. Free education, lazy and willing women, a few good drinks here and there, and . . . I guess there wasn't much else to write home about.

Three days later, I rode in the back of another town car—of course, it was provided for me—down to my summer class.

Johnny, *my driver*, pulled up in front of the building housing my first class for the day, and I swung my Adidas-clad feet out into the bright sunshine. The buildings weren't as tall in the Village, allowing some sunlight to sneak inside the shady city. It made living here somewhat tolerable.

Standing tall outside the car and hoisting my backpack over my shoulder, I allowed myself a moment to think of home. It was early summer—the sun would be burning hot, the crops tall, the trees lush and green. The dogs would have the opposite of spring fever, lazing in the shade around the pond in the heat of the day, and Moira and I would get lost in each other at night in the bed of my pickup truck, underneath the stars, kissing and touching and fucking.

Moira. I took a deep breath and closed my eyes. As I heard Johnny pull away from the curb, I felt every pedestrian stride by in a New York hurry.

Moira didn't want to come with me. She was a small-town girl, not even equipped for Hershey, the closest city to our small town in Pennsylvania, let alone Manhattan. I didn't blame her for not picking up and leaving all she'd ever known for me. Even though we'd promised forever to each other.

All the same, I tried not to think about her pushing me to leave, insisting I experience everything life had to offer, including other women.

In the beginning, I'd waited for her to call and take back her insistence for me to fuck around, enjoy life's riches, and then come back to her. When she didn't, I started screwing my way through every weekend. It's what she asked me to do. Then I'd come back to her, ready to settle down.

Hey, I'm a twenty-three-year-old man, and I'm pretty certain she isn't so innocent herself.

Last I heard, Moira had been going out with the Anderson kid from the other side of town. His parents worked in corporate; he was a good catch, temporarily.

This little adventure in New York didn't take away my plan to go home, live where I always lived, and make a life on our farm, doing what my stepdad had done.

Another horn blared, and I shoved any thoughts of Moira to the far back of my mind.

With my hand no longer calloused from hard labor, I pushed the heavy door open and made my way toward class.

CHAPTER
THREE

Emerson

My head hurt. It ached and pounded. And my mouth? *Ugh*, it felt like it was full of sawdust.

"Ouch." I brought my hands to my head and massaged my scalp, trying to stop the pain.

Once I'd rolled out of bed, I stumbled to the bathroom, peed, and started the coffeemaker next to the toilet.

Yes, you heard right. My coffeemaker is next to the toilet, wedged between the sink and the toilet tank. For the past couple of weeks, I'd been renting a tiny studio apartment in a building in Jamaica, Queens. Really, it wasn't any more than a bedroom with a bath, that bathroom doubling as a kitchen. It wasn't much, but I was making it work.

When I first got here, I spent most of my money on cheap hotels, dead-end bullshit, and some stupid, no-name PI who probably wasn't even legit. He hosed me—but what did I expect? I found him through a Google search.

Oh, and my phone's data plan was draining my reserves. I should have disconnected it . . . all it did was remind me of the pain I was causing my dad. Between his concerned texts and Robby's checking in, I'd never felt so bitchy.

This wasn't me.

By the middle of June, I finally had to admit I wasn't getting anywhere, fast or slow, so I took the remaining money I had left and settled in Queens. The owner of a Bangladeshi restaurant took pity and hired me a few days during the week, and I bartended opposite nights in a swanky joint over in Astoria. It was the tale of a million cities to me, but it was better than wasting a college education.

Oh, the final kicker: *I put school in New Jersey on hold.*

My dad was never going to speak to me again. I'd let him know through text. Was there any other way?

Since I got here, I'd started counting the minutes until Robby moved to New York. He was going to attend a pre-med program where he got a bachelor of science degree and worked toward a medical degree at the same time. It had like a 0.5 percent acceptance rate, and Robby was hot shit, so obviously, he got in. It helped he was from a Podunk beach town where hardly anyone ever escaped. That's exactly why I'd hitched myself to his star.

He was a good choice. A smart choice.

Life in Sea Isle had been good, but I wanted something bigger. Clearly, serving Bangladeshi food that I couldn't pronounce and slinging booze wasn't it either, but it was my current status.

My cell phone rang, and I strained my ears, trying to determine where it was. It rang a second time, and I realized it was in my back pocket.

"Hello?" My voice came out still drunk and raspy.

"What's up, Em?" My name rolled off Robby's tongue, laced with sugar, lining a warm white mocha.

Thank God I paid the phone bill.

"Um, I'm just waking up. Worked late last night."

I lowered the lid and plopped down on the toilet, watching the tiny raindrops of black coffee drip into the glass decanter. My eyes were trained on the Mr. Coffee logo as I listened to the same speech I'd heard from Robby last week.

"I don't know why you're so insistent on that bar job. You could come home, make peace with your dad, and take a few credits in New York or wherever you want, be near me. I'm not saying go full-time in Jersey or anything . . . I just want to see you do right. So does your dad. You'd be the first one to go to college on your side of the family—"

I blew out a loud breath and interrupted his monologue. "My mom went to college, so I'm not the first."

"She's not your family, and you know it. This is some phase you've dragged everyone around you into. Your dad is busy at work, and I'm getting ready for the next ten years of my life. Can't you see that? This is crazy. Your dad needs you."

The smell of the coffee was barely scraping the surface when it came to my headache.

"I'm not making up with my dad right now. He pushed me into this, and now you two are best buddies. What's up with that? I had this fight because of you, because of us. I left Sea Isle because he wanted us to act like prudes, and now you're on his side. Honestly, I don't get it."

I put the phone on mute and cleared the phlegm from my throat, not wanting to share any more weaknesses with the man—boy—who supposedly cared for me.

"Babe, after the phone call we had a few nights ago, there's no way you're a prude. I don't think your dad wants his face rubbed in it, that's all. He's just a dad, overprotective of his girl. And I think you'll want a degree at the end of the day. It's the respectable thing to do."

"Don't," I said sharply. "You talked me into the other night. With all you tell me what you want me to do, and this is a safe place, and I love you, blah, blah. Were you tricking me? Because, frankly, I don't know who the hell you are."

Classic Robby. Always straddling the middle, he confused me. Whose side was he really on? Maybe I was wrong staying tied to him?

"Emerson, what's wrong with you?"

"Don't go all judgy on me, Robby. I'm going to find my way, maybe find my mom, ask her why the hell she didn't want me, and then I can think about school. On my terms. As for making up with my dad, I don't know. He's so unhappy with me . . . like you are now, all of a sudden." My head pounded with each word. "But until I figure shit out, I have to bartend and serve food. It's the only kind of job I'm qualified for, and these people are nice, interesting, different, and not judgmental. I need that."

I scrunched my forehead during the tail end of what felt like a sermon. My head roared at me when I stood too quickly to grab my mug from the medicine cabinet. Finally, the sound of the hot liquid swishing around in the pot was almost as soothing as ibuprofen.

"That's not the way it has to be. I met with your dad the other day—"

"Why? Christ, what is up with you and my dad?"

"Because it's the only way he knows you're okay, Em, and he deserves that . . . don't you think?"

Squeezing my eyes shut, I tried to stabilize my mood. I told myself not to be upset with Robby. My intentions weren't entirely genuine either.

"You're a good guy, Robby. I appreciate you taking care of my dad. But I'm fine. I have a few leads left, and I just want to put this whole thing to rest. Then I can move forward—you know, really grow up, lose my V-card to someone who cares, not worry about getting pregnant and ending up like my mom. God, you and my dad should have more respect for me. I did good in school, and I've not exactly been a fuck-up."

Robby sat there in silence, so I went on. "I can't believe I'm saying this all over the phone, and you're ghosting me on the other end."

"Look, I get it, Em. I do. But we were all good the way we were. Yeah, I wanted more, but we were good, and I was happy to wait. But now you're acting like a bitch."

"What did you just say? I'm super hung over, and I swear you just said I was the one acting like a bitch."

"I did."

"You know what? My dad was so worried that I'd become my mom, that he kept me from going all the way with you. Even though I already feared the worst happening. Yet, now you side with him. Don't you want to be with me? You certainly aren't acting that way."

Christ, I was all over the place emotionally. I started sweating, and alcohol oozed from my pores, filling the air with its putrid scent. Even though I was only eighteen, when we closed the bar, sometimes we had a few libations. It was fine. It wasn't all the time, and our boss turned a blind eye.

"Emerson, I think you need to go sleep this off and talk to me when you're in a better mood."

"So, you don't want to sleep with me anytime soon?"

"Not like this. You say it like you're some cheap two-bit whore. Don't you want to make love like most girls your age? Think about that," he said, and then hung up.

No, I didn't want to do most things like girls my age. I'd grown up dramatically different.

Anyway, *there goes that*. Apparently, I'd been saving myself for a grade-A prime asshole.

After turning over every clue I had so far on my mom, I accidentally struck gold in an upscale bakery on the Upper West Side. By chance, I'd gone in for a cookie and came out with the whole damn cake.

Sweaty and tired, I went to the counter and ordered an iced mocha and a peanut butter and jelly cookie. I didn't know what that was, but I wanted to try one—who knew when I would see a PB&J cookie again?

A cool painting hung on the wall behind the counter. I squinted at the design, painted in slashes of blues and creams and greens, and realized it was an abstract of a coffee cup, steam swirling around it, then funneling into small crescent-shaped cookies.

"I like the painting," I said to the girl at the counter while I waited for my drink.

She glanced back to see what I was looking at. "Oh, that? My mom's friend did that . . . not that she wanted to, but we begged."

"Oh yeah, it's good. Seems like there should be one in every bakery and coffee shop in town."

"Could've been, but the artist doesn't paint anymore. She used to do these big, uppity, abstract things until depression hit big-time. She's one of these upper-class, high-strung, everything-has-to-go-their-way types. Aack, I didn't say that, 'kay?" She pushed an errant dark blond strand of hair behind her ear, her half-moon-shaped earring glinting in the light.

"Your secret's safe with me. I never met anyone like that, but I gotta imagine it's a pain."

"Ha! It is. You got that right, but this is New York, so those types are everywhere. Anyway, the painting is fine. It's only coffee and cookies."

"Too bad, I love it. For the first time since I left home, I actually miss it . . . the ocean air. Something about that painting makes me think of the little beach town I'm from. Maybe the colors, or the way the cookies are floating like clouds above the water."

"She was obsessed with the beach. Paula, the artist, I mean. She was forever going on and on about the sea and wanting to be near water."

She made eye contact with me, but I couldn't focus on her. I didn't know if it was the name she said or the weird itchy feeling on the back of my neck. It felt like a mosquito had gotten caught between my shirt and my neck. Oddly, the urge to get closer to the painting froze me for a second, like I was wearing ankle weights. I couldn't or wouldn't, but then my feet moved on their own, taking me toward the painting. I had to see it for myself.

"You want your drink?" The bakery chick rounded the bar and set it at the end where I was leaning over the counter, trying to get a closer look at the painting.

"Geez, do you want to come back here?" The girl poked my arm with her blue-painted fingernail.

"What?"

"Obsess much? Do you want to come back here? See it up close?"

"Can I?"

She lifted the counter and I slipped through, my gaze never leaving the swirling crescents.

"I'm Bev, by the way, Bev Brantley. You an artist or something?" She leaned against the giant espresso machine.

"No, but I like art. I'm supposed to be studying biology in the fall, but I'm not. I may take a gap year or whatever."

"Oh?" Bev raised an eyebrow at me. It popped over her navy-blue eyeglass frames, and I took a moment to study her. She must be around my age. Green eyes, dark blond hair tied tight in a bun, glasses, and long tanned legs. She looked like a misplaced beach bum, and for the briefest second, I ached for my dad.

My gaze traveled back to the painting, and I reached out a finger to air-trace the first name of the artist's signature—Paula. Then I blinked at the Dubois that followed it, fully convinced I was imagining it.

"My mom's friend Paula . . . they've known each other their whole lives. Except my mom married some broke musician from Brooklyn, and Paula got a fancy art degree and married up, if that's what you call new money when you come from old money." Bev waved a hand in the air. "Jeez, I don't even know your name, and here I am rambling on and on."

"Emerson. It's Emerson."

"Oh, cool name. Bev is so blah. Of course, my mom wanted to be a librarian a long time ago. She loved books . . . Beverly Cleary, Judy Blume, and I forget the other one . . . Roald Dahl." She snapped her fingers when the right name came to mind. "But she became a baker when my dad left on tour and never came back. Someone had to pay the bills. This is her shop. And that's my life story." She waved her hand like Miss America underneath the sign.

Lucky Artist Bakery

"She named it for all the artists who actually made it. The ones in the MOMA and performing at Carnegie Hall. My dad always thought it was about him, wishing him luck. Idiot. Thank God he's long gone. Who the heck has patience for that?"

I slipped out from behind the counter, picked up my drink, and took a sip, desperate for something to do with my hands. Otherwise, I'd grab the painting and run. Where? No clue.

"My mom left us," I said, my hip resting against the counter. I didn't dare share that she might be the same Paula who grew up with Bev's mom.

Bev rolled her eyes, still leaning on the expensive machine. "Well, they suck. My dad and your mom."

I stared at this girl who had been dealt a shitty hand, just like me. How could she have it so together? I was falling apart at the seams, and she was the picture of togetherness, going on and on to me, some stranger, like it was no big deal.

"I never really knew her. My dad's a bit protective. I actually flew the coop this summer because I couldn't take it anymore. All his rules. This is good, by the way," I told her, lifting the drink in my hand.

"Thanks. Sounds dreamy. Flying the coop, that is. My mom got the big BC." Bev pointed at her chest. "Well, I couldn't stand to leave. So I teach dance and work here, running things for her when she's at chemo."

"I've been bartending and waitressing, doing okay, but I need to look for something more permanent."

"Hey, that's about as permanent as you're going to get in this town without a fancy diploma. And even then, it may be your best bet. Where you from?"

"Sea Isle City, New Jersey. Beach town. I guess you could say I'm a small-town girl. That was the appeal of your shop. Had a homey feel to it."

"My mom will be so glad to hear you said that."

"So, the painting. You have more?" I tilted my head toward the only connection I'd ever had with my mother.

Bev shook her head. "No. Paula did this one as a favor to my mom, when she still went by her maiden name. Later, she named herself something fancier—Paula Phillip. But, really, she mostly curated for the museum and then she got into teaching. In the big leagues, not elementary art or anything like that, but at the college, you know what I mean? Last I heard, she was on an extended sabbatical. I don't know what for or what she was doing. She and my mom were fighting a lot over the last few years, but my mom wouldn't tell me over what either. Pretty much, I run the bakery and dance . . . and mind my own business."

"I'm sure your mom didn't want to trouble you. That's how my dad is."

"Prob," she said, turning her gaze toward the door and the bells chiming as it opened.

"I guess you've got to go," I said.

My pulse quickened at the thought of googling my mom again. I wasn't sure why her art never came up, though. Maybe because she had a new name?

As I turned away, I said, "Hey, you said Paula married up. She still married?"

Bev looked at me, her brow wrinkling in confusion. "No, I don't think so. I don't know what happened. She hitched herself to some high-society prick, and it pretty much changed her for the worse. My mom never felt the same about her—it's really sad. I always guessed that's why they fought. I think they lost touch."

I nodded like I understood this type of stuff.

"Supposedly, a lot of shit went down," Bev said with a shrug. "I guess they weren't meant to be or something. And her work signed with her old name wasn't worth what it should've been or whatever. Hence that painting on the wall."

I waved at Bev in thanks, and she grinned back and then took the orders from the couple who'd just walked in and were drooling over the bakery cases.

Excited to have a new lead—a really good lead—I pulled out my phone. According to Google, Paula Phillip was a part-time art professor at a well-established college in the Village.

CHAPTER
FOUR

Price

Collège had never really been a possibility for me. Financially, my mom couldn't swing it, and my stepdad needed help on the farm. Not to mention, I didn't really care about it. I was all too thrilled to oblige my stepdad after he'd put up with my shit for so many years.

Sophomoric, yes. By the way, I knew that word long before moving to New York. I might be a country guy, but I'm no idiot.

A little *Footloose*-ish, you betcha. And, yes, I've seen that movie—both versions—with Moira in my lap, under a blanket, her hands wandering.

Bottom line, it was hard to see myself doing anything else but dairy farming alongside Bruce until he retired. I'd always pictured marrying Moira. We'd have a few kids, buy the farm from my mom and Bruce, and live the way I'd grown up. Quiet. Peaceful.

Except, my kids would have their biological dad.

I'd grown up just fine on that farm until my sperm donor showed up, dust blowing around the tires of his chauffeur-driven town car while he tossed around bribes. I imagined money burning as the driver left the car running.

Now, here I was sitting in a classroom, listening to some highbrow professor drone on about macroeconomics, Apple versus Dell computers specifically, while nineteen- and twenty-year-old girls whispered all around me. Not in the mood for it, I stood to go, packing up my shit in my backpack.

"Hey, one sec," a redheaded beauty with a set of fake tits called to me. "Here."

She shoved a slip of paper into my hand. Her number, probably, but I never got to open it because the prof called me out.

"Have somewhere better to be, Mr. Barnes?" he asked, one eyebrow raised.

I shoved the paper back into the redhead's hand and looked up. "Not feeling so hot. I'll get the notes." I half saluted Professor Sykes and made my way up the stairs and out of the lecture hall.

The hallway was quiet, which was a beautiful reprieve from life in Manhattan. I took a moment to drink in the solitude, yearning for wide-open spaces, blue skies, and a cold beer while sitting on the tailgate of my pickup.

I'm too old for this crap.

"But this type of opportunity is like lightning in a bottle."

My mom's words echoed in my brain, making me want to shake my head until they rattled the hell out. Leaning back into the wall, I closed my eyes and breathed in the silence. My heart beat steadily, and I swallowed any regrets I had about accepting this college education and the apartment—essentially, a chance at having more in life than the farm.

My mom wanted me to be better than Bruce, than her. What she didn't consider was she'd tried that route, shacking up with my dad for a few years, and what did she get out of it? A toddler and a bruised ego.

Pushing off the brick, I made my way down the hall and the stairs to the exit. With an hour until my next class, I decided to grab a sandwich. I burst out into the sunlight just as a tiny raven-haired tornado ran right into me.

"Shit. Sorry, I didn't mean . . . I mean . . . I didn't see you," she mumbled. In painted-on jeans, a black tank tied on the side in one of those knot-type things, and the requisite bright-colored Chucks on her feet, she struggled to find her footing.

I didn't know why, but my hand moved to swipe the long black hair out of her face as she stood. There was a shit ton of it, falling like a curtain in front of her delicate features. When she looked up, staring back at me were a pair of green eyes the color of sea glass, equal parts bewildered and determined.

"You okay?"

She nodded.

"Need help?" I asked, despite seeing she was fine and didn't need anything.

"No. Are you okay?" She ran her hand up and down in the air, motioning at my body.

"I'm fine. Would take a lot more than a skinny little thing like you to do damage to me." I mimicked her hand waving, swiping my large mitt in the air, motioning up and down her body.

"Okay, then. I'll just be on my way."

It was then I realized I'd been holding the door open this whole time. We were half in, half out of the building.

"Be my guest." I waved for her to enter, and then I somewhat sadly exited.

That was it.

Good-bye and good luck, sweetie.

Slouched in the back booth of one of those froufrou café places a little later, I pulled out a book and bit into my egg and turkey bacon on an English muffin.

Yes, you heard me right. 1. Egg. 2. Turkey bacon. 3. English muffin.

It was like one of those riddles on the SAT—which, by the way, I wished I hadn't taken on a whim in high school, because it made this whole NYC bullshit that much easier.

Which two of the above three things does not belong?

If you answered numbers two and three, you win. *Ding, ding, ding! Winner, winner, chicken dinner!*

Who the fuck ate turkey bacon? Not a soul where I came from. And an English muffin was a poor excuse for a biscuit.

Just as I sank my teeth into the last bite of nourishment—because turkey bacon couldn't possibly be classified as delicious—someone took the table next to me.

Not one for coffee-shop talk, I took a swig of my OJ and lowered my face deeper into my book.

"*Cannery Row*? We read that in high school," a female voice said, interrupting my quiet time.

"Hmm." I nodded without looking up, desperately trying to maintain invisible boundaries.

The smell of fresh coffee filled my nostrils, making me think of my mom. She loved her morning coffee. Every day, she made a big pot and drink her first mug on the wraparound porch, sometimes wrapped in a flannel blanket.

"You okay?" Another interruption.

Looking up, I found the black-haired beauty who'd run into me earlier. "Yeah, why?" Slapping my worn book on the table, I suddenly had beef with the pixie extrovert.

"You were reading, and all of a sudden looked really sad. Sorry, I didn't mean to pry. It's just . . ."

I swallowed, wondering how the hell I looked sad, and then I remembered I was thinking of my mom. *So I miss her. I'm no less of a man. It doesn't make me a mama's boy.*

"I'm cool," I said, rather than explaining the truth.

"We just saw each other." She paused, obviously wanting to chat more, and I nodded.

"You go to school here?" I finally asked.

"No. It's nice, though. I was just looking for someone in that building. Didn't find her." She whispered the last part to herself. Only listless for a second, she brightened back up. "Are you a grad student?"

"Ha," I barked. "What? I look too old to play the part of undergrad?"

I was on the bench seat of my booth, my feet kicked out in front of me; she sat opposite me, on the chair side of her table. I wondered if her feet even touched the floor. Compared to my six-foot-two-inch frame, she'd barely hit my chest when we collided earlier.

"Um . . ." She looked away, pink rising in her cheeks.

Leaning forward, I ran my palm over my scruff, trying to remember when I last shaved. "Returning adult student is what I think they call it. School wasn't really in my cards before, and now it is. So here I am."

Sitting quietly, she didn't respond, just raised her brows as if waiting for more of an explanation.

I didn't give her anything more. My story wasn't all that interesting, anyway.

Finally, she gave me an embarrassed smile. "Sorry . . . God, that's all I seem to say to you. I moonlight as a bartender. People just usually seem to want to tell me their troubles. I thought you might."

"Nope, not this person. I don't."

"It's just, you look a little older than the average undergrad. That's all," she said, still pecking at me.

"Anyone ever mention you look a little younger than the average bartender?"

"I'll have you know, you only have to be eighteen to legally tend bar in New York State. Ask my boss if you don't believe me."

Eighteen. I had to keep myself from laughing out loud. Covering my amusement with a smirk, I said, "Does that mean you tend bar illegally?"

"Not here. But sometimes back at home, I'd run the bar at Smithy's Seafood, during the off season . . . which, come to think of it," she rambled, clearly on a roll, "it makes it all the funnier that my dad wouldn't let me spend the night with my boyfriend, yet I was responsible for serving alcohol at Smithy's." She laughed quietly at herself.

"Sounds like you're the one in need of someone to tell their problems to. Maybe you should sit on the other side of the bar." I raised a brow. "Oh, maybe you can't? Not old enough, right?"

Seeming unfazed, she waved her hand in front of her face, faint freckles peppering her perfectly shaped nose—although she looked far from all Miss Fancy Pants. "Never mind. I don't know what's got into me, chatting to a stranger about my problems. Not really problems. I'm fixing it all."

Without another word, she picked up her phone and began tapping away at the screen.

Something about this firecracker with a long mane of black hair got to me. "I'm not really a stranger. This is the second time we've met."

"I don't think so." She shook her head. "Don't think you've found yourself some desperate little hussy willing to get with the first man who lays eyes on her in this big, bad city. I may be young, but I'm not dumb."

"Whoa." I got up and slid into her booth, sitting directly across from her. "All I meant was . . . it seemed like you needed an ear, and I'd be willing to lend one. Since you can't go to a bar and all that. I'm not even from this big, bad, piece-of-shit city, so maybe that helps."

"Well, I'm good. All good. It was a momentary lapse in judgment. You can go back to your own table."

She waved her hand in a shooing motion, and her tank strap fell down her shoulder, revealing an emerald-green bra strap bright against her golden skin. Suddenly, her eyes weren't the only thing intriguing about her.

Forcing myself not to stare for more than a second, I raised my gaze to meet hers as she yanked her strap back up. "For the record, I agree with your dad. I know all about what teenage boyfriends want to do, and he was right. No sleepovers."

"Apparently, my boyfriend agreed too. So there you have it, Mr. Know-It-All. It's been nice knowing ya." She shoved her phone in her purse and stood to go.

"It's Price," I called after her as she hurried to the door.

CHAPTER
FIVE

Price

"How was your day, Mr. Price?" George, a different doorman on shift, greeted me by the name I'd finally trained them all to call me.

"Interesting, more so than most," I said, tossing him a crumb.

"Really? You don't say." He stared at me, his right eyebrow raised.

"Yep," was all I gave up while pushing the button to call the elevator.

I'd ended up being fifteen minutes late to my next class after exchanging verbal jabs with the chick in the coffee place. Something about her took up residence in my mind.

She was a deadly combo; one I'd never come across. Confident, yet not entirely so. Bold, but not always. Young and wise—somewhat. She was a confusing blend of contradictions, like an injured bird and a deadly stallion. Remember those tube-shaped kaleidoscope toys from when you were little? You'd squint, look into the small peephole, and see a myriad of geometric shapes and colors morphing into some strangely obscure pattern. That was my mysterious girl to the naked eye.

I literally shook my head trying to clear any thoughts of her, annoyed that I didn't even get her fucking name.

Upstairs in my apartment, I tossed my backpack on the couch and opened the fridge to snag a bottled water and an apple. After kicking off my shoes, I plopped on the couch, my jeans sliding on the leather.

"I hate this shit," I mumbled to myself.

Freaking expensive leather and fancy rugs. My body craved the smell of hay and fresh-turned earth. Crunching on the apple, I pulled out my phone and texted my mom.

Hey, Mom, how's it going?

Immediately, the dot-filled bubble appeared. We might have to drive to Hershey for a mall, but we do have Wi-Fi and iPhones on the farm.

Taking another bite of my sorry excuse for an apple, I waited for my mom's reply.

All good here. Bruce is busy getting ready for the apple-picking season. There'll be lots of field trips. How's the big city? School?

I felt my cheeks puff out with my long sigh.

City is strange as usual. School is good. Classes are okay. Wish I was there to help. You good? Taking care of yourself?

Don't worry, I'm good. Moira is going to help on weekends in September. You do your thing.

That's the point: this wasn't exactly my thing. It was my father's thing, a man I never knew. How could he know what I wanted out of life? And where the fuck had he been all these years if he was so concerned about me?

As if my mom could read my mind, she texted again.

Your dad, whether he was around or not, wanted this for you. Take it.

That had been my mom's position since the asshole showed up in the driveway, waving the promise of a degree like holding a bone in front of a dog's nose. Except, my mom was the dog, not me.

"*I know you love to read, and not some bullshit graphic novels. You like to write and have a mind for business,*" my father had said confidently, like he'd witnessed this all firsthand. Which he most certainly hadn't.

I'd given my mom the side-eye for even speaking my name, let alone sharing my interests with this man. Clearly, my parents been in touch without my knowledge, which was a swift punch to the gut.

"*Christ, Price, you don't want to be stuck here on the farm for the rest of your life,*" he'd said. "*Be a filmmaker, an Indian chief, a journalist who travels.*"

I'd stared at the man, not able to conjure up one inkling of similarities between us, other than I could see where my olive skin and thick, dark hair came from. Otherwise, absolutely nothing called to me from this man.

With Moira tucked into my side, her hand pushing into my back, silently telling me to go, take what was being offered, I knew she'd known this was coming. Obviously, my mom had known and told her. Bruce had known and not said a word. It had all been decided before I even knew about it.

I was going to college, the first on my mom's side of the family to go.

Clearly, I wasn't going to be the first *not to go* on my father's side.

I'm going to come home for a weekend too. I'll let you know when.

I sent my mom one last text before tossing my phone on the coffee table.

Lounging back into the couch, I closed my eyes, and the raven-haired beauty came to mind again.

What was she looking for? Why was she bartending at eighteen and not in school? What was that sad look in her eyes when she'd mentioned not finding who she was looking for?

Deciding I couldn't dwell on a girl—especially one I really knew nothing about—I went for a run and came back to my book and a plate of pasta.

CHAPTER
SIX

Emerson

Bev sat across from me at the bar. "Crap, this is a schlep coming out here. I'm taking an Uber home. No E train for me."

"Thanks for coming, though," I said, wiping the bar in front of her.

I didn't know why or what had possessed me, but I'd stopped at the bakery this week to say hi. I guessed I liked her; something about Bev drew me to her. I wouldn't say this aloud, but she felt like home to me. Plus, I didn't really have anyone else in this big city, so I sought her out like a bee to honey.

This past Wednesday, when I didn't have to bartend until five, I'd spent some time in the city searching for Paula Philip since my lead at the college didn't pan out, and suddenly found myself hangry for a cookie. I'd gone to the bakery, catching it during a lull, and Bev and I had sat for an hour, just laughing and, and it felt good. When I'd told her about my two jobs, she'd promised to come see me at the bar today. I'd promised to sneak her in, and here we were.

"Place is nice, though," Bev said, looking around. "Yuppie crowd. Bet you make good money."

"It's decent. What can I get you? It's on me after you *schlepped* all the way out to Astoria." I rolled my eyes in jest, checking on Trey, my supervisor and the head bartender. He was busy making an Instagram post, which would take him ten minutes until he got it just right.

"Whiskey sour, extra cherries."

I tossed a napkin labeled TVRN on the table in front of her and grabbed a lowball glass. "Interesting choice in drinks."

"Eh, seemed fitting, plus it's been a shit day. I need something to knock it out of me."

"What happened?"

See? Like I told that douche back in the bakery, people love to tell bartenders their problems.

Setting her drink in front of her, I said, "Spill it. It's quiet right now." I looked at my watch, noting it was a quarter to five. "We won't be for long, especially on a Friday."

"My mom is bad again. Found a lump under her arm. They don't know what it all means, and she's a wreck, trying not to show it. But I know. I just know she's a mess."

Leaning on the bar, I rearranged my messy bun and listened. "That's rough. What will they do next? I don't know your mom, but she sounds like a fighter. She'll attack this."

Bev took another sip of her drink, sniffing back her fear and the impending onset of tears. "Surgery, maybe chemo."

"Ugh, gotta be rough. I can't imagine something like that happening to my dad . . . even if he's been a dick."

She blinked several times, swallowing hard. "All she has is me to take care of her, but she wants me to go stay with a friend, so I don't have to see her like that. I can't do that. You wouldn't, would you?"

"Of course. I mean, I don't know what it's like to be close to a mother, but yeah, you need to be there for her."

She nodded. "Okay, enough about that. It's off my chest. Tell me more about the crowd that comes in here. Hot? Sexy as fuck? Any good-lookers in their early twenties? For me, of course." She waggled her eyebrows above her eyeglass frames, and I couldn't stifle my laugh.

Good-lookers in their early twenties made me think of Price, the prick who hadn't been nice, but then was. I'd met two people in this city. One was sitting in front of me, and the other didn't even know my name.

"We'll get a good crowd tonight. You won't be sorry you came. I swear."

I poured myself a Diet Coke just as the bells over the door jingled and the music started to pour through the speakers. It was five o'clock on a Friday, officially happy hour, and the TGIF crowd was filing in.

Smiling, I told Bev, "Have fun, girlie," as I prepared to make several hundred drinks. "Oh, watch out for the bunny," I added with a wink, and poor Bev squinted at me, her brow furrowed. I didn't offer any further explanation. She'd figure it out soon enough.

At the end of the night, Bev stayed with me as I counted my tips and had a drink. "Oh. My. God. I had no idea what you meant when you mentioned a bunny. Who the hell is that? And what is that all about? I've lived in New York all my life, and I never." Bev laughed into a glass of water.

"I told you to look out for him. Apparently, it started back in the Village years ago, probably when we were babies. A guy named Frankie would dress as a bunny and hit on all the female customers in the bar. He was apparently pretty famous there, and when he got older, his son took over. Being a poor New Yorker, he moved to Queens. His name is . . . wait for it . . . Frankie Junior."

I released my hair out of its messy bun, scratching the nape of my neck where it was itchy from a few too many hairs pulled tight.

After several rounds of laughter, we made small talk in the afterglow of a good night for all, including Frankie Junior, who'd danced with Bev. She'd flirted with him and everything else that moved on two legs and had a penis, and I'd raked in the cash.

For a while tonight, we both forgot about our moms. Bev needed to forget because she ached all over at the prospect of losing hers. As for me, I ached all over at the prospect of finding mine. We were opposing ends of the same continuum, thrown together by some random stroke of kismet.

As I sipped a vodka and tonic, I somehow knew my not telling Bev the truth would haunt me, but I couldn't bring myself to say it. The multitude of ways this whole Paula thing could end were too great, and I wasn't sure if I wanted to share that with anyone just yet.

When we were finished, I waited with Bev for her Uber before splurging on a cab home.

With my cheek against the cool pillow, I didn't think of Robby. A dark-haired, sort-of-older (which made everything more questionable) guy had taken up residence in my mind, and I wasn't sure how it made me feel, other than happy.

CHAPTER
SEVEN

Price

S aturday afternoon, I kicked back in my apartment with a cold beer and my book—*Cannery Row*—hiding from all the Big Apple had to offer.

I'd read the plotless story several times, and it was still my favorite. Sad, how it became truer and truer to my own life. Rather than the cannery employees, we were the struggling, down-and-out farmers. Then there were the people in the surrounding big cities who had chosen a different life. Except now, I was caught between the two worlds.

The doorbell knocked me out of my reverie, and I made the mistake of opening the door without looking through the peephole first.

"Hey, Price. I'm house sitting this weekend for my aunt, and I was wondering what you're up to?"

It was Monica—a mistake from when I first moved here. With Moira's harping on me to sow my wild oats ripe in my mind, a bruised ego from my mom pushing me to this place, and a momentary lapse in judgment, I found solace in the girl down the hall. Grateful to learn she was only house sitting for her aunt who lived in the building, I'd sworn never to shit where I ate again.

Now as she leaned against the doorjamb, wearing a black crop top and even blacker leggings outlining her camel toe, her feet bare, I recalled why I don't sleep with neighbors (or house sitters of said neighbors) anymore.

"Having a low-key weekend," I said, trying to avoid long moments of direct eye contact. I'd learned my lesson . . . city girls weren't like the girls back home.

"You should come out! It's Saturday." She leaned forward, her fake tits on display, bouncing with her every step.

I knew all about them . . . her dad bought them for her on her eighteenth birthday. I'd had to bite my tongue in an effort to resist laughing at that. *Tits for a birthday gift!* Apparently, it wasn't uncommon around these parts. Can you imagine?

On my eighteenth birthday, I got gift cards to the wing place and the gas station, and an *"Attaboy, now you're a man"* from Bruce.

"Thanks for the offer, but I'm probably going to stay in."

"Nooo. You can't. This building is so lame. It's so quiet, I can hear the clock ticking. You need to come out with us. It's a group," she said coyly, twirling her hair between her thumb and forefinger, a duck face replacing her smile.

"I'll think about it," I said to get rid of her.

"Oh, great. I'll come by around nine and we can share an Uber, then grab everyone else. It's a plan."

"I'm not a definite."

"See you later," she said over her shoulder, already sashaying her ass down the hall.

Happily alone again with my book and my beer, I spent the rest of the afternoon on the couch.

A little before eight, I opted to head out and pick up some food, trying to avoid Monica and her Uber. With a bag of cheap Chinese takeout tucked under my arm, I grabbed the keys hanging from my mouth to unlock my apartment, hoping I was safe.

"Priiiice! Woo-hoo, let's go!"

"I'm not really feeling it, Monica." I waved my bag of takeout in the air. "Plus, I'm in ratty jeans and a flannel. I'm sure you don't want to be caught dead with me. I hardly scream New York's finest."

"Are you mocking me?" She looked at me, her head tilted to the side, her breasts rising and falling with each breath, her eyes wide.

Shit. I didn't mean to make her feel bad.

"No," I lied.

"Come on, let's go. We're going to Astoria to see the bunny. No one cares what you're wearing. Eat your food later tonight. Just leave it in your apartment."

"Okay." I turned my key in the door, shoved my food in the fridge like she said, and locked back up. I couldn't insult the woman and then not go, especially when she was giving me a second chance.

"A bunny?" I asked when we got on the elevator.

"Yeah, Frankie. He's so, so, soooo fun! He used to hang in the Village, but he's found a new home in Astoria."

"A real bunny?"

"No, silly." She pinched my cheek and leaned forward to playfully brush my nose with hers, filling my nostrils with her overly vanilla scent. "A cross-dressing bunny. You'll love him."

There was no appropriate response to this.

We picked up two other people in the Uber, a girl and a guy from the Upper West Side. "Mandi with *just* an I," and "Sidney, not Sid."

Fucking New Yorkers. They always scream their uniqueness.

"Price, *just* like what something costs," I said by way of introduction, unable to resist running my smart mouth.

We sped out of the city, over the bridge, and through the streets of Queens until the Uber pulled in front of a restored building, the letters TVRN painted onto a faux-worn trim. Right away, I could tell this was one of those froufrou places pretending to be a shithole.

After Sidney, not Sid, paid for the Uber on his app, we all volunteered to pick up the ride home, and off we went. A large bald guy stood at the door, handlebar mustache, rock band T-shirt stretched across his chest—could he be any more cliché?

"Cover is twenty-five for the guys, nothing for the ladies."

Of course.

Pulling my worn leather wallet from my back pocket, I shoved a fifty into the guy's hand. "I got him too," I said, jerking my head toward Sidney.

When we walked inside, I saw I was right. Bourgeois disguised as a shithole.

"Come on." Monica tugged on my shirt. "I see a table." She hustled as if her life depended on it to a misplaced farm table.

"Why are we in Queens again?" I asked. "When we live near a thousand bars?"

Monica rolled her eyes. "It's fun to go slumming, like the Village back in the day."

"What do you know about back in the day? You're about as fresh-faced as they come."

She slapped my arm. "Stop! Come on, let's have fun!"

My head shook on its own. Of all the ideas, this was close to the dumbest.

I ran my hand along the table's finish, too glossy to be from a farm, too smooth to have ever been in a real working-man's kitchen.

"First round's on me," Sidney declared as I sat my ass down in an uncomfortable chair. "What'll you have?"

"Ooh, I want a margarita on the rocks, definitely Patrón, and yes to salt," Monica said without even looking up at Sidney. She was fixated on her own cleavage, adjusting her tits just so.

"I want a Moscow mule," Mandi said. "Don't you love those mugs they come in?"

"Bottle of beer for me, nothing too rich for my blood," I said.

Sidney sneered at me. "Coors Light?"

"Nah, I don't do light. That's for wusses."

This got his ass moving toward the bar, and I settled back in my seat, taking in the place.

A DJ spun loud music in the corner, eclectic tables crowded the floor, light bulbs strung from fake barbed wire hanging from the beamed ceiling, crown molding lined the perimeter, and a long shiny wood-grain bar stretched across the back wall.

Chuckling to myself, I watched Sidney jockeying for position at the bar while Monica and Mandi discussed their outfits as though they'd been called to the White House and their matching crop tops were of the highest security scrutiny.

Poor Sidney was waving his hand in the air, desperate for the attention of a bartender, when finally, a pint-sized thing called him over. Her dark hair was piled on top of her head, strands of it flying everywhere, a tight royal-blue tank top stuck like glue to her perfect chest.

Lifting my gaze back to her face, I recognized her. There was my galloping stallion, looking proud, working in Astoria.

How 'bout that?

This night instantly became much more interesting.

"Here." Sid shoved a green glass bottle in my direction and set two sloshing drinks on the table. He took a healthy pull of his draft beer—I'm sure some yuppie IPA bullshit—before moaning about the line at the bar.

"I'll do the honors next time," I said, happy to offer.

"Fine with me. So, did you scout any fine fish in the sea while I was gone?"

"What?" I couldn't help the eye roll. "We're in Queens. There's willing and able girls everywhere, but no fine fish in the sea."

Except for the girl behind the bar. Who was definitely more than just willing-and-able snatch. Way fucking more. Yep, I knew this from our few minutes together. She was one tough nugget, curious mind and eyes, bold and timid at the same time.

Make no mistake, I'd have her number and her story after tonight. There was something about that one—she was different from the others, and she didn't seem to know it. I'd noticed a slight shadow of pain behind those sea-green eyes, and while I didn't like the way it made me feel—like I wanted to take it away—it drew me in anyway.

"Oh, I love this song! Dance with me." Monica tugged on my arm, bouncing to the techno beat. She was up and out of her seat in no time, teetering on her heels. "Let's go," she whined, and I begrudgingly accepted.

I was barely moving in place, obliging Monica with the full-body rubdown she was attempting to choreograph, when I looked up and caught *her* gaze. Her being the girl—young woman—whose name I didn't even know yet. She was watching from behind the far end of the bar, her eyes lasered in on me and the woman trying to paint me with her scent.

I shook Monica's arm, trying to get her out of her reverie, and said, "I gotta go to the bar." It was lame, but so were her trite pickup lines and unoriginal moves. I wasn't just some dumb farm boy.

As soon as I was on the move, the girl pretended to get busy. Real busy, stuffing glassware on and off the automatic wash machine. She kept her gaze down behind the bar and continued to slam, soak, rinse, and shove each glass onto the drying rack.

"Hey, can I get a drink?" I played it cool despite the fact that I'd been sweating about this mysterious girl all week.

Her head lifted, along with her right eyebrow—cute as hell. "Can you? Or is it time for you to return to the senior citizens' home?"

I felt a smile tugging at my lips. "Soon, but not before you get tucked in for the night. You still need one of those, right? Do you like milk and cookies with your tuck-in?"

"Touché. What can I get you? No—let's see if I can guess. Scotch on the rocks for the returning adult student? Or maybe high-end vodka and soda for his distinguished palate?" Her gaze did a quick trip to my chest and back up. "By the way, what's with the flannel? You trying out various 'I'm not really a rich New Yorker hipster looks,' or are you just slumming it?"

Her messy bun flopped backward with her giggle and air quotes. It made me want to reach over the bar, snag her damn hair, pull her over to me, and show her just how *not* hipster I was.

Whoa, cowboy.

"You're awfully judgy tonight," I said. "Skip dinner? Forget your vitamins?"

"Nah, I just call it like it is. Had stuff shoved down my throat for way too long. Turning over a new leaf, and all that jazz." She waved her jazz hands, mocking her own words.

"Got it. So you've been had, and now you'll have anyone in your way."

"Scotch or vodka, pretty boy? Leave the analysis to the paid help."

"Beer, whatever's your special. Cheap and easy's actually my drink of choice."

She bent down and pulled a bottle of the same brand I'd had earlier out of the cooler and popped the top. "Here ya go, Price."

I can't even get into what my name on her tongue did to me. It was inappropriate in forty-nine states.

"Thanks. You're a piece of work . . . oh, right, I don't even know your name, young lady."

"I know." She winked.

Some random rap blared in the background, and I'd never felt more out of place.

Tossing a few bills on the bar, I turned to go, my ego reassured with the knowledge I'd be back for more. "Actually, I wore flannels before the hipsters did. That's what we did back home on the farm. Of course, only after we spent all day actually doing real work."

Her mouth hung open. She should learn not to always judge a book by its cover. I suspected that was a big part of whatever issues she had going on, but I had time to teach her.

All of a sudden, I wasn't so fucking pissed to have been uprooted to this piece-of-shit city.

CHAPTER
EIGHT

Emerson

Imagine my surprise when I looked up and saw the star of my recent fantasies grinding on the dance floor with some trashy model wannabe.

Okay, okay. He wasn't the one doing the grinding, but really . . . what the hell were they doing in my bar?

Just like that, he spotted me and made his way over, and what did I do? Insulted him some more.

Now he was walking away from me, and I wanted to yell, "Come back. Please!" Luckily, another crush of people swamped the bar, and I needed to either serve drinks or get mauled.

"What can I get ya?" I called into the crowd, and just like that, Price was lost in the sea of people.

The orders dragged on—whiskey and soda, rum and diet, two IPAs, a pale ale, vodka and cranberry, a million mules—until finally "the song" came on. It was from before my time, but I knew it. Not from here, but from my dad.

Silly, but at the mere thought of him, my heart hurt. My dad. Everything between us was so mixed up, but I didn't have time to dwell on it.

The pineapple song blared through the speakers, and there he was. Frankie strutted his stuff around the bar, lifting his leg and groping men and women alike. The crowd was already halfway to bombed, and everyone was into any and all of it.

Everyone except for the object of my attention.

No, Price watched with a half smirk and leery eyes as the cross-dressing bunny captivated the room. The music changed, and Frankie still did his thing. Customers vied for his attention, especially the chick who Price was dancing with earlier.

If she was the type of girl he went for, there was no way I—the Virgin Mary—remotely had a chance with him. All I had was an overactive imagination that seemed to play well for phone sex.

"So, is this an every-night thing?"

The question knocked me out of my thoughts, and I found Price standing in front of me, an empty beer bottle in hand.

"Who? The rabbit?"

"You working here. How many nights a week do you do this?"

"Oh. Want another?"

"I asked you a question."

"Not all of us can do as we want—go to school, hang in bars, have fun."

He leaned close, his forearms on the bar, his breath hot on my cheek. "I think you're making some heavy assumptions for a not-quite-ripe bartender, don't you? I mean, you haven't been doing this so long, have ya?"

He was so near and all man, testosterone and some type of masculine musk practically wafting from his pores. If I'd ever thought Robby was a real man, I was wrong. Robby was a sheep in wolf's clothing.

"What did you say?" It's the truth. I hadn't heard a word he'd said.

Price moved closer, leaning over the bar, and his lips tickled my right ear. "I said . . . I think you're making some heavy assumptions for a not-quite-ripe bartender, don't you?" He pulled back the tiniest of tiny bits and watched me swallow, his gaze following the visible lump going down my throat.

Rather than answer, I pulled back and bent down to grab him a beer. After popping the cap off on the back edge of the bar, I handed him the ice-cold bottle and wiped my hands down the front of my apron.

"A little different from Smithy's Seafood?"

He remembered what I'd said. *Interesting.*

"Little bit, but I can hack it." I held my chin high.

"This your main gig then? Bartending-slash-counseling the masses?"

"I waitress too. Over in Jamaica. It pays the bills."

"I know all about that. Paying the bills. That's what I did before I went back to school."

He took a long pull of his beer. I became mesmerized with his mouth and the small shadow of scruff surrounding it, the swallow of beer sliding down his throat, his Adam's apple bobbing.

"Listen, I didn't mean to make assumptions. I'm just a small-town girl living in a big-city world." I swallowed whatever pride I had left. After all, I'd already told this guy about my dad and Robby.

"S'okay. You got a name, small-town girl?"

"Emerson."

"Em," he said quietly just for him and me, reaching out to run a finger down my cheek. "I'd like to utilize your counseling skills on a night when you're not here . . . overtime, if you will. There's dinner and dessert involved. What night are you free?"

"Hey, if you're not gonna order anything, can I get two IPAs?" Some ass wormed his way up next to Price and shouted to him and me.

"I gotta work," I told Price.

"Which night are you free?"

He's determined. I'll give him that. Let's face it, I wanted to go.

"Monday?" I asked.

"Give me your phone," he said before turning to the asshat scowling. "And for your patience, your drinks are on me."

"Thanks, buddy. After monopolizing the help, it's the least you can do."

"At least she'll get a bigger tip out of me."

Price grabbed my phone and entered his number before calling himself. "See you on Monday, Em."

How did I have a nickname already?

Sunday dragged by without a word from *farm boy* Price. Monday arrived with more dreaded silence.

Oh well, I told myself.

Except, I really wanted to cry or some other girlie stuff. Eat ice cream. More crying. Doodling our names together on a notepad. Then more crying. Who was I to know what sad girls usually did? My father certainly never taught me.

Instead, I slept in until the sun was high in the sky. After all, I'd had yet another sleepless night. With only one eye open, I made coffee next to the toilet, spent some time on the internet researching my mom, and then slung Bangladeshi food for six hours.

Sometime in the middle of my shift, I took a fifteen-minute break to pee and have a plate of chicken curry, and I finally saw a text.

Sorry for the delay. Phone crashed & I had to spend all yesterday in the dreaded Apple store. Let's plan for 7 tonight? I'll Uber to you. What's your address?

Like he thought I was going to give him my address. Please—I wasn't that young and stupid.

Will meet you at the restaurant. Where do you suggest? Somewhere with an early bird? Is 7 too late?

They were stupid, overused quips and lines, but even over text, this guy scrambled my brain.

You like Italian? I asked around & there's a good place in Astoria. It's Monday, so prob no wait. Trattoria V.

He didn't even acknowledge my snark.

And he'd asked around? What the heck did that mean?

I had no witty comeback, plus I needed to get back to my tables. I'd need the tip money for an overpriced Italian joint. I assumed we'd go Dutch . . . that's what I'd always done with Robby.

Sounds good. See you then.

That was all I could come up with.

Oh yeah. You will. ;)

Oh boy. One winky face later, my stomach was doing jumping jacks and my heart was sprinting down the street.

I needed a reality check, and lucky for me, I walked right out of the break room and into a coworker carrying a tray of curried rice. Covered in spices and tiny sticky grains of rice was enough to make me stop and smell the coffee, or the harsh reality.

I was so fucking far out of my comfort zone, I didn't even know the name of the game I was playing.

CHAPTER
NINE

Price

I could have called Johnny, but judging by Emerson's early impressions of me and her quick assumptions, taking my personal driver wasn't a good look.

I'd Uber to Astoria, and hopefully, she'd let me Uber her home. After that, anything else was wishful thinking.

Yesterday was a real clusterfuck when my freaking phone died. Thank some fucking deity that I added that whole cloud backup shit for school, and I was able to get my contacts back. Standing in the Apple store, I was sadly turning into one of those needy, whiny, self-serving New Yorkers.

"Sir, I need my phone. I need a phone. I need all my stuff on my phone. How much longer do I need to wait? I really need my phone."

Need, need, needing all the time.

At home, we all had a phone. We texted, called the farm supply store, or sometimes googled shit—mostly porn as teenagers.

Now I needed my fucking phone like I needed oxygen.

One of these days, I was going to hate myself. Probably tomorrow, at the rate I was going.

This morning, I asked one of the richie women in my finance class about restaurants in Astoria.

"Oh, definitely Trattoria V. Ah-mazing!" The girl's strawberry-red hair had flown all around her face as her eyes widened, her eyelashes fluttering. *"But you need a reservation. It's always mobbed. You need to call a few weeks in advance."*

And there I went with needing all over again.

How the hell did I need a reservation to an Italian restaurant? They were a dime a dozen in this city. A joint, no less, that I wouldn't have even dreamed of being caught dead in six months ago—let alone being able to afford?

Fucking Christ.

I imagined my mom crossing herself as I took the Lord's name in vain.

Fuck it. I didn't have time to worry about my mom.

I explained to Strawberry Shortcake that it was for tonight, and I didn't have weeks to call in advance.

"Today's Monday." The girl had turned her nose up. *"Who goes out on a Monday? You'll be fine. Just go there."* Then she'd huffed her way over to her seat, in a tiff over something—maybe me not asking *her* to the Italian place? *Come on . . .*

Now I sat in an Uber, my palms sweaty for the first time since I felt up Sharon McKinley behind the barn. It had been smooth sailing for me back home. Couple of pull-ups on the bar across the stable doorway, toss a few barrels of hay for the obliques, add in football and track, and *bam*—get any girl you want.

Not so much here in the Rotten Apple. Here, you needed to work at it, make money, work out, make reservations. Though, I didn't think Em was like that—she was something else altogether.

The car came to a stop in front of a corner restaurant, complete with a black awning with the name of the restaurant in white lettering, brick-lined steps to the door, and a valet. Money and garlic wafted from the doorway of Trattoria V, and I'd never felt lesser.

After tossing a ten to the Uber driver, even though you weren't supposed to tip, I slammed the car door. The guy probably had a family of four and moonlighted as an Uber driver while I was playing Richie Rich on Central Park South.

At least I'd been wise enough to wear dark jeans, no rips, and a button-down. The boots couldn't be helped. It was either boots or Adidas—which were new for me. I'd adopted the sneakers after being transplanted to this strange city. No matter what, I wasn't ever going to be a loafers guy.

I turned to look down the street as a lone figure made her way up the sidewalk, wearing tight-ass jeans, ankle boots, a flowy-type shirt baring one shoulder, and her long dark hair a wild mess from the windy night.

"Hey there, old fogie," Emerson said, greeting me with a smile.

"You take the subway?" I couldn't help the indignation in my voice, but there was no way I'd ever want my date to take the subway alone at night, even in the summertime when it was still light outside.

"Yep. Not all of us can Uber around to fancy dinners on a Monday."

"Yeah, this place isn't really my speed. I asked a girl in one of my classes. I should've known better, but I wanted to impress you," I said, adding a wink.

"Oh yeah?" Emerson's eyebrow raised, and I noticed a small scar above her eye. I wanted to run my finger along it and ask her how she got it.

"Let's try it, though. I got all dressed up," I said, trying to lighten the mood—hers and mine. "When in Rome . . . or whatever they say. I've never been to Europe."

She ran her fingers through her wind-blown hair, looking at anything but me.

I tried to picture what we looked like. Two complete strangers on a street corner, indecisive and hesitant, attempting to make a plan.

"You okay?" I asked.

"Um, this place. It's sort of out of my comfort zone, let alone my budget."

This made me laugh. "A, this place is so far out of my comfort zone, you have no idea. And, B, I don't know what it's like in . . ." I snapped my fingers, trying to remember where the hell she was from. ". . . Sea Isle City, but where I come from, the guy always pays on dates."

"Oh," was all she responded, and I couldn't hold back my surprise.

"Wow, just *oh*, nothing else? No sarcastic wit?"

"I'm going to have a moment of clarity right now, and since you already know my most embarrassing story, I'm not going to get upset over this. But here's the thing. That's the first time anyone—man, guy, or girl, for that matter—has ever said anything like that to me."

It couldn't be helped. I ran my hand down her arm, the soft fabric not catching on my now smooth hands. I tucked the memory back in the recesses of my brain.

"Well, there's always a first, and I'm happy to be it. Now, let's go eat at this place that's supposedly so good, and hope we're not hungry when we leave."

Her gaze met mine, all her fears, insecurities, and emotions swimming in those green seas. "Can you afford it?"

I laughed again. "Yeah, sadly I can. Tell you more in there." I jerked my head toward the awning, took her hand, and led her to the restaurant.

Inside, I told the hostess, "Two. I called earlier. Barnes." Pathetic, but I did call.

The hostess busied herself, tapping away at an iPad.

"I didn't know your last name," Emerson said.

"Now you do. And yours?"

"Bender."

"Right this way," the hostess said.

"They're both Irish," I said as we sat down.

"Yeah, I guess so. My dad's Irish. Yours? Lay it on me." Emerson rested her elbows on the table and leaned forward, her eyes open and welcoming.

Shit. I shook my head, clearing it of my crazy touchy-feely thoughts.

"What?" Her green eyes looking almost blue today, encouraging me to bare my soul to her.

"Do you ever let a person breathe?" I took a sip of the water and almost spit the shit out. "What the . . ."

"It's sparkling." She laughed at me, or with me, while patting my forearm. She quickly removed her hand, but not without staring for a second at her fingers, as if she were surprised at their forthrightness. "So, tell me."

We were interrupted again by the server, asking for drink orders. I ordered a beer and Emerson a diet pop. *Excuse me. Soda.* When the server left, I paused for a second, choosing my words.

"Here's the short version. My mom met my dad when he was doing some kind of internship in Philadelphia. He'd come to Hershey to meet with some smaller companies. She was a young, easily impressionable, blue-collar girl, smitten with the handsome guy from out of town. Of course, he took advantage, and she became his main squeeze while he was in the States. Then he went back to where he came from, but not before knocking her up. Apparently, he was the son of an Irish guy and an Arabic woman. A forbidden tale of its own . . . I don't even know it or care. My mom knew way back when and told me some of it, but I never really paid attention. Anyway, she kept me, and he stayed out of the picture until recently."

Emerson sat quietly, her gaze intent on me throughout my whole monologue. When I finished, I took a gulp of my hideous sparkling water, wetting my tongue and cooling my emotions. I'd never laid it on the line like that before.

The server brought our drinks (*thank God*), along with a basket of bread and a bowl of olive oil and balsamic vinegar. I waved him off.

"My dad kept me," Emerson said quietly. "Even though my mom didn't want me."

"I'm sure he's a good man like my mom."

She shrugged. "A bit overprotective."

"Already told you, I'd tend to agree with him."

"So, what happened? Is he back? Your dad?"

"Nice way to deflect. And, yeah, he drove down our driveway one day in his limo, waving money and promises of a free education, demanding that I be more than an ordinary farm boy. Apparently, he'd kept up with me, knew all about me. My mom had stayed in touch with him, never expecting anything in return. All I wanted was to run the farm with my stepdad, Bruce, but here I am in the Big Apple, set up in some posh apartment with a healthy allowance."

"I'd say it all sounds pretty nice." Emerson looked up, an eyebrow raised, one side of her red lips upturned. "Independence, freedom, bills all paid."

"Eh, it kind of sucks. Well, up until now."

"Oh, really? I can't be that much of a salve."

"We'll see about that, Bender."

This got me a full smile, her white teeth on full display.

"Wow. Who knew that calling a little lady by her last name would get such a reaction?"

Her smile dulled a bit, and she stared at the white tablecloth and rows of silverware. "Back home, my dad's friends call him Bend. I know I've pissed him off, and I feel bad about it. He was strangling the life out of me . . . but he also gave life to me. Lord knows, my mom didn't. So I'm torn. And my old boyfriend, he apparently is an ass, and now he's moving here. It's everything I originally wanted, but now I'm not sure."

"Sounds like you need a bartender."

"Sorry." She swirled the straw in her soda. "I tend to ramble when I'm upset."

"That's what I'm here for. The rambling." I reached out and stilled her hand with mine.

We were quiet for a few beats, and it was calming in a way I hadn't known since coming to this city. Her without a mom, me without a dad, both searching for a slice of the elusive happiness pie.

"Hey," I said, "want to blow off this joint and grab some pizza?"

If I'd thought her smile was big before, this time it was epic.

"Yes!"

"Done." I tossed a twenty on the table and said, "Something came up," to the server, and we were out of there.

On the street corner, I asked Emerson if she knew of a place. She didn't, but she pulled out her phone, quickly finding somewhere on Google.

We walked side by side to a dingy pizza place, where we demolished a large pie. I ate of most of it, but she didn't act like one of those high-society New York chicks who only drank sparkling water and ate lettuce.

We laughed about Trattoria V, and how we wouldn't be caught dead in a place like that back home. I told her about the farm, milking the cows and picking apples. She listened wide-eyed.

"I'd love to see that one day. Sounds so cool," she said, and it seemed genuine.

She told me about the beach in the winter, when it was quiet and desolate, almost lonely. Like mine, her high school only had about a hundred students in four grades.

"Then summertime comes, and the place is swarming with people. Restaurants are packed, garbage cans overflowing, and lots of money to be made," she said. "It's cool because you get to meet lots of different people from all over, I guess . . . that's what my dad always said."

We wiped our greasy fingers on paper napkins and guzzled down syrupy fountain sodas until it was way later than we realized.

"Shit, it's almost eleven," she said, glancing at her phone. "I have to work a double tomorrow, daylight at the restaurant and nighttime at the bar."

"I'd like to Uber you home. No expectations. Just want to make sure you're safe. Is that okay?"

"Sure you do." She sort of laughed, but I wasn't sure she was joking.

"Scout's honor." I put my right hand up in the air, and she narrowed her eyes at me.

"You're not walking me up to the door. Just the car ride, and off you go."

I nodded in agreement, but I was lying. I was kissing her good night at the door. Or maybe in the car.

CHAPTER
TEN

Emerson

I couldn't help it. I woke up the next morning running a finger across my lips like a lovesick fool in a romantic dramedy. Oh, wait, that's exactly who I was.

Price had stayed true to his word, remaining in the Uber, but he paid the driver to keep the meter running and he kissed me. Right in the back seat of some stranger's car . . . close mouthed, but not one bit tentative. No tongue, yet more sensual than I'd ever been kissed before.

Maybe I was naive, but his kiss had felt full of promise and emotion. A promise I didn't have to return, yet I gifted myself a few more seconds of reminiscing about his lips on mine.

And then it was over, and I was full speed ahead, starting my day. Coffee, shower, then wait tables.

When I finally finished with the lunch rush, I saw I'd missed a call from Bev.

"What's up?" I asked when I called her back from the break room.

"What's up with you?"

"Working. You know, living the great American dream."

"Yeah, I feel you. Anyway, I was hanging with my mom during one of her treatments, and I told her how much you love Paula's painting. She has another one in the back of her closet. You want it?"

"Um, how much does she want for it?" I tried to temper the buzz of excitement jolting through my veins.

"It's for you. Nothing, if you want it."

"I can't take it. Your mom probably wants to keep it anyway."

"Emerson, I said you could have it. Hey, why don't you come up to the bakery later in the week, and we can go for happy hour?"

"Oh, okay. Thursday?"

"Good. Okay, gotta run and get my mom some broth."

"Tell her I'm thinking of her. I mean, even though I don't know her."

"I know what you mean. See you Thursday."

She disconnected the call, and before I could put my phone away, it buzzed with a text.

I'm coming up to meet with my adviser next Tuesday. See you then?

Robby. *Shit*. I'd forgotten all about him in the last twenty-four hours. Obviously, he wasn't that important. Or as important as I'd made him out to be. Whatever.

With no clue how to respond, I shoved the phone back in my pocket.

Later that evening, on the brink of early in the morning, my phone went off again. Back in bed, I was tempted to ignore it and close my eyes.

Anger swelled in me at Robby. How could he demand my attention next week when he'd basically sided with my dad?

Setting my anger aside, I checked the phone and found a text from Price.

Thinking of me?

Actually, I was, but I wasn't about to admit it to Price. Instead, I set my phone to DO NOT DISTURB and went to sleep.

I was sure there must have been some dating rules as to when and where and how and what I should reply to Price. With zero patience for looking them up or googling what I should do, when I woke up the next morning, I fired off:

Just counting the water marks on my ceiling & waiting for the coffee to finish.

He responded right away.

You sure make a guy work for it.

For what?

A second date. What did you think?

Coffee's ready. Gtg. Text next time you're on my side of the water.

After flicking my screen off, I buried myself under the covers and wished what I'd said about the coffee was true. *I should go home* was floating through my mind, but I was too stubborn.

Finally, I pulled myself out of the sheets and made coffee and went about my daily routine, trying to forget it all—Price kissing me, Robby coming to town, and missing my dad.

"Michelob," was shouted at me from across the bar.

"We don't have it. Try an IPA or something from the draft board," I hollered back without looking up, continuing to make the drink in front of me.

"What's that?" the familiar voice asked, still pestering me.

"Gin fizz."

I knew who it was, and I wasn't in the mood to deal with how Price made me feel.

"I'll take one of them. Make your life easy."

"A gin fizz? That's what you're gonna drink? You?" I finally looked up, catching his messy hair, sneaking out from the hood of his sweatshirt. It was old, and probably just the right amount of worn-in soft.

"Sure, why not?"

I held up a finger, signaling for him to wait a sec, and delivered the gin concoction down the bar. When I came back, I said, "Because it's a craft cocktail, and you consider yourself a small-town dude."

"Surprise me. Make me whatever you want. How's that?"

"What are you doing here?" I leaned on the bar, eyeing him up, my attitude covered in a fresh coat of badass. In reality, I wanted to crawl into his sweatshirt and go somewhere quiet with him.

"Me?" He pointed at himself with his thumb. "Getting an adult beverage."

"Aren't there like twelve-point-two bars and restaurants per block up where you live?"

"Twelve point four, but who's counting?"

I grabbed a shaker and mixed a surprise for Price, sticking a cherry in the finished concoction.

"Mmm." After taking a sip, he licked his lips, raising an eyebrow in question.

"Sex on the Beach."

"Perfect. Not my kind of drink, but definitely would be my kind of sex . . . I'm guessing on that, by the way."

"Guessing?"

He blinked, his eyelids closing over his blue eyes for a second. "Never been to the beach."

"Never?"

"Never. Nope."

"The other night when I was telling you how I'm from a beach town, you didn't say a thing," I said.

"I didn't want to spoil your story. You looked so happy talking about home."

Christ, he was right. I was so happy thinking about home.

"Hey, want to take care of some other customers," some prick yelled.

"Wanna take me to the beach?" Price asked before he knocked back the remainder of his drink.

"I have to go help them." I tilted my head down the bar.

Waving his empty glass at me, he said, "Then come back, because I don't have a drink anymore."

I poured a couple of brews, mixed a margarita for some girl with a permanent scowl and a bad nose job, before snagging a bottle of beer and placing it in front of Price.

"Heineken. I'll make do." He took a sip with me watching the liquid roll down his throat. "Eyes up here," he said, and my cheeks burned.

"So, tell me, what are you doing back here tonight?" I shoved a flyway hair behind my ear and grabbed my water.

"Wanted to see you."

"No funny pickup line or made-up excuse?"

He shook his head. "Not my style. At the risk of you laughing, I'm still going to ask. Want to come over my way this weekend? Eat, and then walk through the park?"

Of course, he didn't work two jobs to make ends meet, but his life circumstances weren't his fault. "Um, I work Saturday lunch."

"No prob. Sunday?"

I nodded, tongue-twisted, words lost to me. Was he for real?

"Great, it's a date," he said, smacking the bar. He threw down a fifty and tossed me a peace sign.

"I can't—" I tried to protest, but he was already out the door.

CHAPTER
ELEVEN

Price

My feet hit the pavement in even strides. Heavy, humid air hung around me, and I ran a hand over my face, swiping the sweat out of my eyes. A horn blared in the background, less abrupt than the pounding in my heart. Not from exertion, but from the thought of kissing Emerson the other night.

Fuck. I didn't know why I was so caught up about it. I'd had plenty of women since leaving Moira and home. We had an arrangement. Then I'd gone and visited Em at work . . . and it became clear that anything with her would be above and beyond the arrangement Moira had in mind.

The sound of horse hooves rang off to my left as I made my way down Central Park South. My first mistake: I'd abandoned my earbuds for my own thoughts. They plagued me all the way back to my building.

"Hey there, Mr. Price. How was your run?"

"Better now that you got my damn name right, Rudy. Now if you'd just drop the *mister*, we'll be right as rain." The last part came out with a hint of twang, and it made me hungry for a plate of farm-fresh eggs and thick-cut bacon.

"Management's rules." He held a hand up as if taking a vow. "If I could, I would."

"Yeah, yeah," I said, taking the chilled bottle of water he offered me. "Whose life is this?"

"Excuse me, sir?"

"Sorry. It was a rhetorical question. At home, I'd be drinking from the garden hose."

This got me a chuckle from Rudy. "I'd love to see you do that here. You'd be getting a lot of strange looks, even from the dogs."

I chugged the water, then crushed the plastic bottle.

"Haven't seen you around much when I've been on evenings."

Leaning on the desk, I said, "Been going out a little bit."

"Well, that's good. Means you're adjusting to your new life."

"Not sure that'll ever happen." Lifting my arm, I swished the crinkled-up bottle into the garbage can. "Three points!"

"Ready for the Knicks, Mr. Price!"

"Knock it off," I said with a smile.

"Okay, ready for your new life here in the city."

"Still not sure I'll ever be ready."

On my way toward the elevator, Rudy called after me, "We'll see."

And I was right back to thinking about Moira.

Unable to shake her from my thoughts, I decided to call her. It wasn't bacon and eggs, but her voice was the next best thing to being home.

"Hey, what's up, Price?" Somewhat breathless, she answered on the second ring.

"Nothing's up, just checking in."

"Oh."

"Is everything okay? You sound winded." Setting the iPhone on speaker, I took off my wet T-shirt and plopped down on the couch. I probably wasn't supposed to sit on the expensive leather all sweaty, but I didn't really give a fuck.

"Yeah, everything's fine. I'm working in the farm store today, and I was in the back dealing with inventory."

"It's been a while," I said, not knowing what I wanted her to say back.

"We haven't talked in a while, and I . . . I think it's good. You're doing your thing, and I'm doing mine. Well, mine is the same thing I always did. Which, don't get me wrong, I want to do. I like it here. I'm happy here."

"What's really happening?" I ran my hand through my messy hair, mentally berating myself. It's not like we'd decided to stay together.

"I just think you should really move on. You know, move on, move on. Sorry, that was a lot of move-ons . . . this is harder than I thought. Look, you got out. You're getting a fancy education. It's not like you're coming back here."

"Moira, I plan to come back. I want to come back. This is good for me, though, to get a degree, make my mom proud. But this isn't forever."

Despite what Rudy said.

"I know, and I want you to do it. It's just, you're experiencing life in a way I may never, and I don't know how we could ever make it work after that. Do you understand?"

"No, I don't. We have history, planned a future together. What the fuck . . . heck . . . is this?"

But did we have a future? Emotions tugged in my belly, and I didn't like it. I liked feeling self-assured. That's what being back home felt like—confident. New York felt like a punch to the gut. So did this phone call.

"Look, Price. I know you're as loyal as they come. If we'd decided to be faithful while you were away, you would've been. I didn't ask that of you, nor would I. We're young, and we both deserve to experience life wherever we may be. But it's time for you to cut the cord and really live there. In New York. Not calling to catch up or any of that. Got it?"

"This is crazy. What would you have done if I didn't call?"

"You woulda called. That's you. And I still love you, Price."

"Um, it sure doesn't look that way from my vantage point," I said, realizing what a hypocrite I was. Who the fuck was I to feel that way? I'd been walking around dazed over Emerson.

"I do. I care for you more than anything, but we—all of us here—we know you're not coming back. Your mom too. And we had an arrangement. I told you to go off and experience the city, and I'm sure you have."

"What is this? An intervention?" I balled my fists and blew out a breath rather than punching a wall. "And my mom? Jesus, she's in on this too? How about this . . . we'll see," I said, echoing the same words Rudy had said to me ten minutes earlier.

For once, I wasn't absolutely sure if I'd go back home. I wasn't sure who I was or wanted to be when this was all over. I didn't know what I wanted to do.

Other than see Emerson again.

Yes, it made me a dick, but I wasn't the only bad guy here. Moira had fucking ended a lifelong friendship over the phone, making me wonder.

Who the hell was she fucking?

I knew Emerson wouldn't be happy, but it wasn't in me to give any fucks. Which is why I smirked at eleven on Sunday when I got a text rant from her.

There's some dude at my door saying he's your driver and he's here to take me to your place? I'm capable of making my own way there. And who is this guy anyway?

He's safe. Go with him.

I didn't text any more information or details. She'd go with Johnny. I knew it.

After a shower, I tossed on clean athletic shorts, and then changed into khaki shorts. Sifting through my clean laundry bag, I found a faded blue T-shirt and pulled it over my head, leaving my hair rumpled.

The buzzer rang as soon as I finished pulling the blanket over the bed, making it look halfway decent, and I grabbed the phone.

"Hey, Rudy."

"You have a visitor, Mr. Price."

Certain Emerson was laughing, I cringed at his name for me. "Yep, one sec. I'm going to come down and get her, 'kay?"

"Certainly. I will entertain Miss Bender for a few minutes."

That's exactly what I was worried about. I tossed the phone aside and hurried downstairs to get Emerson.

"Hey there, Mr. Price," I heard as soon as I stepped off the elevator.

"Funny," I said to Emerson before whispering to Rudy, "You can't help a dude out?"

"Here to serve," Rudy whispered back.

"Come on. Let's go upstairs and get this over with," I said as I stole Em's hand.

"Nice meeting you, Miss Bender," Rudy called after us.

"Over with?" she asked me when we got into the elevator.

"I'm sure you'll have some comments regarding where I live. So let's get it out of the way, and then we can go on with our day."

She turned to face me, her long legs going on for days below her denim cutoffs. The strap of her sheer white tank fell off her shoulder, and her hair was down and wavy.

"Touchy?" she asked, smiling.

"You smell good." I pulled her close, breathed in the top of her hair, and conveniently changed the subject. "Like sunscreen and coconut."

"It's from home, a beach body spray."

The door opened, and we stepped off in sync.

"Now I can say that I know what the beach smells like with authority."

"And I can say I know how the rich live with authority."

"Here we go . . ."

I pushed the door open; I hadn't bothered to lock it. Who was going to get by Rudy without an inquisition?

"Home sweet home," I muttered as Emerson made her way into the apartment.

"Wow." She approached the floor-to-ceiling windows and placed her palms on the glass. "This is so insane. You can see the whole island."

"I like to look out over the park and map my runs." I came up behind her, placing my hands lightly over hers.

"Look at all the horses." She took in the smelly parade of carriages carting tourists around the park.

"Only thing that makes me feel like I'm home."

"Oh, right. Do you ride?" She turned around, leaning back against the glass.

"Yes. I don't love it. Not my thing. Back home, I ride an ATV a lot of the time."

She sneaked under my arm and explored my apartment, picking up trinkets I didn't buy or had no use for. "So, what's the deal? You live here rent-free? Do you ever see your dad?"

I settled my back against the window and closed my eyes. "Pretty much. I live here. I own it. My dad put it in my name, which is . . . gah, so fucking emasculating." Which summed up how my life had been going.

"Why? He obviously cares for you. That can't be such a bad thing."

"Look, I don't want to be rude. You can ask me anything. But this just isn't my favorite subject. My mom worked hard to raise me, and I always thought I'd be some hardworking provider. Now I live like a douche and don't do a thing."

She set down whatever knickknack she was studying and approached, leaning into me. "Got it. But think about it. You're in school, and you will do something, so maybe that will take some of the pressure off. I wish my mom would've come back for me."

Her forehead found my chest, and we stayed liked that, my heart pounding into her ear. It embarrassed the hell out of me, but she didn't say a word about it.

"My dad doesn't come around much. Said he had to deal with an emergency, but I would be well taken care of. Must've been one hell of an emergency, because I haven't seen him since he left me here."

"Well, it's a cool place, but I think I got one up on you with my toilet-slash-shelf for my coffeemaker."

With one little quip, the serious mood was broken, and we were laughing in each other's arms. It was the first time I'd felt relaxed in this city full of concrete and hardened people.

"Want to go eat?" I asked Emerson, mesmerized by her complete lack of . . . I don't even know what to call it. Lack of being impressed with any of this shit?

"Yes. Where to?" she asked while I grabbed my keys.

"Want to go down to Chelsea Market?"

"Oh yeah. I haven't been over there yet. Is this okay?" She waved a hand in front of her outfit.

"Yeah, why?"

"It's not designer or anything, Mr. Price," she said with a wink. "Can I go like this?"

"Shut it," I said, texting Johnny. "Let's hitch a ride there and then make our own way back, later?"

"Sure," she said, fidgeting with her hands, twisting her fingers together.

"Look, I don't want to try to hide this. I have a driver. He doesn't have anything else to do, so let's have him take us," I said, unable to help my defensive tone.

"It's cool. Look, I'm not judging. We all have our shit."

Johnny was waiting outside when we pushed through the heavy doors onto Central Park South. I told him where to drop us, and he pulled away from the curb without comments or questions. Small miracles do happen.

Emerson's phone buzzed, and she asked, "Do you mind if I grab this?"

I shook my head, and she swept her finger over the phone.

"What's up?" She looked out the window as she listened, nodding. "Oh, that sounds great . . . Glad your mom will be there . . . Sure, let me see if I can get the day off. I don't want to make too much work for her . . . Um, okay, I'll text you."

After quickly disconnecting the call, Emerson smiled like I'd never seen her smile before. Granted, we'd only spent a few times together, but suddenly, irrational jealousy raged just beneath my skin.

"All good?" I asked, tempering my feelings at whoever the fuck put the smile on her face.

"Oh. Yeah. That was my friend Bev. She runs her mom's bakery. It's cute. We should go there sometime." Like creamer in coffee, her comment lightened my mood. "Anyway, they're having an art show next Friday, and she invited me. I've been wanting to meet her mom, and she'll be there." Her eyes turned almost blue, excitement sparking in the normally light green orbs.

"You like art?"

"I do," she said, looking away. "I think so, at least. I'm figuring that out lately. Bev's mom knows a lot of art people, and a few may be there. I can ask questions, mingle, figure it out."

There was something she wasn't saying. Emerson was hiding a thing or two, but I didn't push. After all, I hadn't been up front about Moira or my original plan to go back to her, or my reticence to admit I was somewhat happy with Moira's dismissal of me.

Deciding to let it go, I wanted to live in the here and now and savor this decent moment in this dreaded city I'd been plopped down into.

Johnny dropped us off on the corner near Chelsea Market, where the buildings were markedly less vertical and the vibe less severe. I felt my breathing get a bit easier. My dad could have at least taken time to know me, understand my likes, help me find my own way in this city, rather than just deposit me where he did without any input from me.

"This place is just the right amount of hipster. Not too garish, zero feel of old money, but casually hip, yet not overly hip," Emerson said, rambling as we made our way down the aisles of Chelsea Market.

I turned to her and lifted an eyebrow. "Casually hip?"

"What? I like to really understand a place. So, kill me," she said, holding her hands up in surrender.

"You do work with the bunny! I mean, you're sort of casually hip—"

With a pretty decent side-eye, Emerson told me, "Shut it."

"I like it here too. Food's all pretty good, and the vibe is just right," I said, giving in and agreeing with her.

We paused in front of a Mediterranean restaurant.

"Wanna try this?" I asked her. "I've been once before, and it's pretty damn good."

"Smells yum. Did you know, vegetarian food is big in a beach town? We have a juice and vegan place on every corner. But I didn't take you for a veggie. More of a carnivore."

"Back at home, I'm all about the meat on the grill, but this shit's growing on me." I winked at Emerson, and with two fingers in the air, motioned to the hostess that we needed a table.

"We only have bar seats right now. That okay?" She waved toward the bar seating, facing the open kitchen.

I looked at Emerson. "You okay with that?"

"Great," she told the hostess.

Seated in front of the hot grill, Emerson scanned the kitchen with wide eyes.

"You like to cook?" I asked her.

"I do. I've always experimented in the kitchen, especially during the long winters. Most of the places close up until the vacation season, so my dad and I ate at home a lot."

"I bet you're a good daughter."

"Nah," she said softly, rearranging the condiments on the counter. "My dad misses me now, and I didn't leave on good terms."

"I'm sure he understands. People fight."

"I did the one thing he asked me never to do. Look for my mom."

"Can I get you guys anything to drink?"

A brusque server interrupted our moment, and I could have sworn I saw relief wash over Emerson's face.

"Beer?" I asked.

"I have a great IPA from upstate on tap," he said, his gaze dropping to Emerson's bare legs.

"Great, I'll take it. Em?"

"I'll have one too."

"ID?" The server eyed her up and down.

"Oh, I forgot it. Never mind," she said with a weak giggle.

His eyes still on her thighs, I suspected he may have served her if I weren't sitting next to her.

"Thanks, buddy. Bring some Cokes too," I said, dismissing Mr. Leery Eyes.

Emerson side-eyed me again when he left. "I think I'm too young to be with you."

"Be quiet. Now, tell me why you think your dad won't forgive you."

She pushed a strand of hair behind her ear, and I noticed the pierced earrings studded along her cartilage. A tiny hand, an evil eye, and an arrow. Obviously, she felt she needed to ward off bad juju.

"He hates my mom, ever since the day she left me on his doorstep and walked away. Not because of me, though. That I believe. He loves me, did the best he could, blah, blah. But he hated her for never coming back, for not realizing her mistake. I mean, who doesn't want to know their daughter? But he didn't look for her or try either—instead, he strangled me with rules and tried to keep me under his thumb."

"Maybe he needed that," I said. "For himself. Maybe he worried you would leave too. Or maybe he worried about you being hurt again. I mean, I'm sure it wasn't easy growing up not knowing your mom. I know . . . because of my dad. I had Bruce, though."

"Well, I did leave. And, yes, it hurt, but not in the way he thought. I didn't feel like I was missing something other than answers. I wanted to know why she did it."

"You're not in Africa or the Middle East. If she wanted to see you, she would've. Not to be harsh, but sometimes you gotta let these things go. And you can't tell me I don't get it."

She shrugged, her shoulders slumping.

"Look, you're only one state over," I told her. "Call your dad, go see him, and make peace. Then come back and look for your mom, if you still feel you want to."

She shook her head. "Not until I find my mom. I don't think she would've left New York. From what I heard, she loved it more than anything. More than me, obviously. But I still want to find her."

"Do you want her to see what she missed? Or do you want to torture yourself with what you may have missed? Or maybe you didn't miss anything at all . . . could it be?"

"The first. And then I want to go on with my life. Actually, maybe a little of them all."

Leery Eyes was back with our drinks, and I quickly ordered some appetizers without asking Emerson for her opinion, wanting him gone.

"Well, then, cheers to you finding her soon. I just wouldn't want you to be chasing a connection or relationship that may never happen." I clinked my glass into hers and took a sip.

"Obviously, your dad thinks he missed out on something . . . with what he's doing. And he's trying to make up for lost time," she said to me while looking at the floor.

"I don't know what my dad's motives are, but they feel more like post-war reparations than genuine feelings. I think it's more a guilty conscience than anything else."

Our food began to arrive, and we shifted the conversation back to less serious subjects.

I told her I was studying business, because what else was there to study? I wasn't going to be a doctor or lawyer. One day, maybe I'd expand the farm, have some sort of bed-and-breakfast type deal going on. Host weddings. Come up with an extra revenue stream or two. I didn't mention Moira, or how a few short months ago, I thought we'd build these ideas together.

Emerson said she was putting off school. "A gap year. Although, no one from where I'm from takes one. They either go to work or school. No one is rich or extravagant enough to do it. I guess I'm working, really. Waitressing. Like him," she said, watching Leery Eyes make his way over with our entrées.

"Maybe you could go to culinary school or do something with food?" I suggested.

"Ha! With what money? My dad isn't paying for me to stay here and traipse around. He was going to send me to college in New Jersey for state tuition. He was cosigning on a loan."

"Take a loan here. I'm sure you could make it all work."

"You've never even eaten my cooking," she said, pretending to punch my arm.

"Well, now I know what to plan for the next time we get together."

"Oh, now I'm cooking for you? Slaving in the kitchen?"

"At least you didn't argue about a next time."

She dug her fork into the baba ghanoush and moaned once she slipped it into her mouth. "That's good."

I wanted to say, "*Not as good as watching you eat it.*" But I kept that to myself.

CHAPTER
TWELVE

Emerson

"**E**merson!"

My name carried through the bar, and I looked up to find Robby making his way through the crowd. Tall, out of place in his buttoned-down shirt and belted khakis, the guy who used to rock my world now only made me feel anger and sadness.

Shit. I forgot.

"I was going to wait until tomorrow, but surprise! I came early." He approached wearing his big, fake smile.

Oh, right. He was supposed to come on Tuesday and today was Monday. I had a legitimate reason for not remembering.

Searching for the right words, I stalled as I shoved back a thick hank of hair that had fallen from my messy bun behind my ear. "So, you decided to find me at work?"

That's the entirety of what I could come up with in a sea of possible responses. I tried to school the anger in my voice, but I wasn't very effective. It felt like Robby was checking up on me, or maybe that was my guilty conscience?

I hadn't talked to Price since yesterday when he—well, Johnny—drove me back to Queens. Price's lips had grazed my forehead as we stood in front of my door. He'd said we'd see each other soon, but I had work and he had classes.

Robby's smile faltered. "Wow. I thought you'd be a little more excited. Cute place here, where you're working. Your dad would love to see it."

"Em!" Randy, my coworker, stood by the flip-up bar door with a heavy bucket of ice, eyeing me, desperate for someone to open the counter for him.

"Coming," I told him, holding up a finger to Robby.

Randy gave me a once-over as I flipped up the door. "You good?"

"Yeah, friend from home."

I turned to go back and meet whatever battle Robby was here to start, but Randy tapped my shoulder.

"Holler if you need me," he whispered.

I nodded and whispered back, "Thanks."

When I got back after helping Randy, Robby had found a spot on a stool and was staring at his phone like it held all the answers. Or nuclear codes.

"Sorry," I told him, but I wasn't. I'd needed the space and the quick break. A month ago, I'd wanted to give him my virginity. Now I found solace in my coworker having my back over any potential blowback of Robby showing up unannounced.

The initial surprise was starting to wear off, and still . . . none of my old feelings for him rushed back. Nada. Zip.

"Want something to drink?" I asked Robby, sliding a menu in front of him.

"I have an ID," he whispered.

Shaking my head, I told him, "It's fine, no one will check. This is Astoria. We serve drinks and make money. We don't police people unless they're falling over drunk or beating the shit out of someone."

"Beer, whatever you have on draft."

I pulled him a draft and set it on a coaster in front of him.

"Your dad's worried and wants to see you," Robby said. "He wanted to come with me today, but I told him I'd check in. You should come home. Give up the ghost, make peace. Paula isn't a part of your life."

"No," I said firmly, busying myself so I didn't need to meet his eyes.

"Emerson, your dad knows he was too strict, that he caused you to run off. But it's only because he cares. Go see him. He wants to make amends. He needs to tell you that he wants us to be together. To give us his blessing. Then we're good."

Stunned, I finally looked up. "Blessing? What, are you crazy? This isn't some arranged marriage. We're high school sweethearts. I wanted to spend the night with you, but I also want to find my mom, and as luck would have it, I'm close. I have some leads." Glaring at him, I added, "You and my dad can't decide my life for me. I'm not some slab of meat hanging in a butcher shop."

"You don't need to find her. I'm the steady in your life. Your dad's the steady. What else do you need?" Robby reached out and took my wrist in his hand, his grasp a little tighter than I liked.

Pulling back, hard, I wanted to ask him where this was coming from, but we were interrupted. And I started to think I might need Randy.

"Hey, leave the lady alone."

The voice came from somewhere close by, and it wasn't Randy's voice. It was Price.

"Shit." This time I didn't keep the obscenities inside my head.

"Mind your own business, dude," Robby said harshly to Price.

"This is my business. Em's a friend."

Robby stood and puffed his chest out. "Is that so? Well, she's my girl."

"I don't give a shit. This absolutely fucking *is so* my business." Price stood tall, no chest puffing required, throwing Robby's words back in his face.

Robby turned to me. "Emerson? Care to explain?"

"Don't talk down to her," Price said, staring Robby down.

Frustrated, I held up my hands. "I have to get to work, Robby. Tell my dad I need closure. Or I will. And thanks for looking out for me, Price. I need to make money, so you two can both go your own ways, and I'll talk to everyone later. 'Kay?"

I snatched Robby's now empty glass and tossed it in the sink before moving down the bar. Yeah, I ran, but this was too much to deal with on a regular old Monday.

The bar's door hadn't even slapped shut behind me after my shift was over before Price was next to me. "You okay?" he asked, his palm on my shoulder stilling me.

"I'm fine," I told him. "Seriously."

"Really?"

"Yeah, thanks for letting me do my thing. Some of us have to work for a living." When he pulled his hand away, I felt its loss more than I would have liked. "I'm sorry. That was a low blow."

"S'okay. You've had a rough night. Want me to take you home?"

"You mean, Johnny?" I asked as the two of us strolled down the sidewalk, going nowhere in particular.

Price's hand found my waist and stopped me in my tracks. His touch wasn't rough or painful like when Robby had grabbed my wrist. It was gentle, if that's a thing. What the heck did I know?

"No. I sent Johnny home and waited here for you. Myself."

"Oh."

"Oh? Who the hell is that guy, Emerson? Is he the one you're holding out for? He doesn't deserve to be in the same room as you, let alone in your bed. Is that who you're running back to or from?"

"He's confused or nervous or something, but he cares for me," I said, stupidly defending Robby.

Price frowned and shook his head. "He's not."

As if drawn like magnets, our bodies met, our feet taking small steps on their own until our chests barely touched, right in the middle of a busy sidewalk in New York.

"Price . . ."

"Em, listen to me. When it comes to you, there's no reason to be confused. To know you, to see you, watch you smile the way I saw you smile on the way to the market . . . the way you're easygoing, but serious when it matters, the passion you feel when it comes to others . . . I promise you, there's no confusion. Not one moment's confusion."

I had no idea what he was talking about, because he didn't give me a chance to ask him to explain.

Before I could take another breath, his lips met mine in a bruising kiss. Closed mouth, urgent, hurried but great. I didn't think he cared we were in public, and I knew I didn't. Having Price's mouth on mine was a luxury I didn't even know I yearned for, yet here I was savoring it.

"I'm not confused," he said when he broke away from me. "I want you, all of you. The *looking for your mom* version, the *upset with yourself for abandoning your dad* side, and everything in between."

"Price, I'm a waitress. And you . . . you're together." That was the only argument I could come up with.

"Come on, Em. Let's get an Uber and get you home."

My right hand tucked in his left, he used his free hand to order a car, some unfamiliar but welcome energy swirling around us.

The next morning, I sat in bed and dialed Robby.

"Emerson, what the fuck?" was how he picked up my call.

"What?" I decided to play dumb. It was early, and I wasn't fully awake. And I was in denial. My personal life was like a storybook run through the paper shredder. All of my early chapters blown to bits, with nothing to show for where I'd been and what I'd done.

With empty pages behind me, it was time for me to write my own future.

"What? You acted like I was a stranger, basically tossed me out of the bar after you sicced your new boy toy on me. What the hell? Have you been pining away for me, or dating half of New York? Which one is it?"

Slinking down on my pillows, I cleared my throat. "Can I talk?"

"Oh, sure, Emerson. Should we add your dad on the call? Because what in the ever-loving fuck am I going to tell him?"

"Can you please stop talking so crass?"

"Why? Does your new guy talk like a gentleman? He certainly didn't look like one with all that wild hair and ratty T-shirt."

"Robby. You're getting ahead of yourself."

"Tell me I'm wrong."

I couldn't say he was, so I stayed quiet.

"See? You can't even defend yourself. What the hell is your dad going to say about this? This guy protects you from me, and you go acting like a floozy in the big city."

"I'm not acting like a floozy. I've made friends, I work hard, and I'm looking for my mom."

"And you're not going to school. Did you know I'm going to be a doctor, Emerson?"

"Of course I do, Robby."

I stood, lightheaded and weak. What the heck did he want from me? He'd sided with my dad, when all this started because of him.

Walking toward the mini bathroom, I decided I needed coffee.

"I can't have a bartender as my better half."

"Wait, what did you just say?"

"You're a bartender."

My ass fell onto the toilet seat. "Yes, I know. I'm paying my bills and looking for my mom."

"You've thrown away everything for her. Your dad really got the shit end of the stick. And I can't exactly be walking around in my pre-med program with someone who isn't even in school to do anything professional."

"Well, I guess you came here for nothing."

"No, I came here to meet with my advisor, remember? I'm going to make something of myself."

"Lots of luck to you, Robby."

I hung up with one thought running through my mind. *Thank God I didn't give him my virginity.*

Maybe my dad was on to something. I needed to call him, figure stuff out with us, and apologize for bolting, but not right now. First, I needed coffee, and then I'd think on it.

With my first sip of joe, I realized Price wasn't wrong either when it came to Robby. Robby wasn't confused . . . he knew exactly who and what he wanted, and it wasn't me.

My hands curled around the warm cup, I found myself alone in a big city, looking for a woman I'd never met, and without the only two people I'd ever trusted.

A chill ran the length of my whole body—a fear greater than any I'd ever known. But with a resolution stronger than the sludge I'd brewed, I peed and decided *screw 'em all.*

CHAPTER
THIRTEEN

Emerson

"Thanks, Randy." I'd stopped in to pick up my paycheck and thank Randy for taking my shift at the bar.

The smell of cumin still hung heavy in my hair from my shift at the restaurant earlier in the day, but I didn't have time to shower and change before heading to the art show at the Lucky Artist Bakery. Bev's mom was going to be there, and she was my luckiest and biggest lead to finding my mom, all wrapped up in one.

Wearing jeans, a loose off-the-shoulder gray V-neck, flip-flops, and a messy bun would be how I would meet her. With a fresh coat of mascara and lip gloss, I looked shabby chic. It was the best I could do.

"Want some food?" Randy called after me.

"No thanks, I'm good," I said over my shoulder, knowing there was no way I could swallow anything past the lump of anxiety in my throat.

Outside on the sidewalk, I made my way toward the subway. I didn't want to be late to the party, but I also didn't want to appear too excited. A fireball of mixed emotions swirled in my gut . . . and then my phone pinged.

You heading to the bakery?

How the heck did Price remember?

And did I want him to know?

Since it was time for me to go underground and get on a train, I decided to answer him when I got out on the other side.

Price had been conveniently busy the last few days . . . after my relationship with Robby had blown to bits. Which was fine, because I had enough shit to deal with, like figuring out how to salvage my relationship with my dad while still looking for my mom.

On my way now. How r u?

The second part I added out of obligation. It was hard to be mean, especially when he'd just taken up for me in a bar a few days before.

Good here. Want some company?

Wow, I wasn't expecting that response. Clueless as to what to say next, I did the easiest thing . . . I ignored his text.

Quickly making my way to the bakery, I went over in my mind what I wanted to say to Bev's mom. Of course, when I finally walked through the door and the smell of fresh-brewed coffee and chocolate filled my nostrils, I forgot every last word.

"Em!" Bev called to me from behind the counter.

My eyes roamed the small shop. People were mingling, some holding hot beverages and others champagne flutes. Bright contemporary art I hadn't seen before covered the walls. A dude in jeans, a white T-shirt, and cowboy boots—presumably the artist—stood in the corner, talking to a group of people.

As I waved at Bev, a woman made her way from the group chatting with the artist and joined her. Smaller than Bev, the woman was wearing a tie-dyed dress, cinched at the waist with a beaded belt, and a bright orange scarf tied around her head.

Bev waved me closer, and my feet moved of their own volition, the breath whooshing from my lungs. Above them behind the counter hung Paula's painting—my lucky break at the Lucky Artist Bakery. The tips of my fingers and toes tingled with fear and excitement.

"Hey, thanks for coming," Bev said while stepping around the counter and pulling me in for a hug.

"Place is packed."

"I know, right?"

Bev's mom joined us. "Hi, I'm Sheila. You must be Emerson. Bev hasn't stopped talking about you," she said to me with a smile.

"Nice to meet you . . . glad you could be here. You know, that you're feeling well enough," I said, stumbling over my words and emotions.

"Me too. Do you like the work?" Sheila waved her hand around the bakery, and I scanned the bright splatter-painted canvases.

"I do. It's fun, cheerful, hopeful."

"That's what I thought, and we can all use a dose of that," Sheila told me.

"You can say that again," I said, without going into the details of my week.

Bev gave me a quick grin. "And they're selling."

"Well, that's good." I looked around again, amazed by a neon painting and then one made up of primary colors. Completely out of my comfort zone, I never thought I'd be at a New York City art show.

"Bev told me you love that one." Sheila changed the subject, glancing toward Paula's painting.

"I do. There's something that makes me feel settled looking at it. At ease."

My phone burned in my pocket as lies spun from my mouth. I wasn't the best version of myself, continuing to ignore Price's text, telling half-truths to my only friend and her mom.

"Did Bev tell you I have another one? Paula painted them one afternoon just for fun for me. They were meant to be a set. Funny, this was long before I owned the bakery, way before the idea of this place even existed. We were two young New Yorkers who liked dessert. That's why she made the cookies floating out like that. We were goofing around, I guess. When we still could. Goof around, I mean." She looked wistful as she spoke, as if she were reminiscing about better days.

I shook my head, still stuck on her initial question. *"Did Bev tell you I have another one?"* I'd never been this close to finding my mom, or at least having more clues.

A chill ran up my spine and landed in the back of my neck. I ran my hand there, massaging out the excitement. Or was it anxiety? Still, I continued to hang on her every word, especially the mention of my mom's name.

Sheila put her hand on her hip and jutted it out like a fashion model before explaining. "Of course, we didn't eat cookies. We were too worried about our curves and dieting. If I knew now that none of it mattered, I'd have eaten the cookies."

"Ha, well, I eat cookies. Bev will tell you that's how we met. Over your PB&J cookie. It's become a weakness of mine." *Among other things.*

"Bonded ever since. All because of a cookie . . . nothing to do with me," Bev joked.

"I'm so happy Bev is branching out and making new friends," Sheila said. "The last year hasn't been easy for her. That's why I said if you liked the painting so much, you could have the other one. Would you like it?"

Biting my tongue, I kept myself from shouting, *"I would!"*

Instead, I said politely, "I couldn't do that. Maybe Paula wants it back. As a memory."

"*Pfft*, no. I haven't seen her in a few years, and I doubt she'd want it back. She left most of her past behind."

"Oh, that's sad," I said, not knowing how to respond, thinking that was the most appropriate thing to say. The harsh reality was that I knew all about how Paula left things in her past. *Including me.*

A couple approached the counter, wanting a sweet treat, and Bev went to help them.

Her mom patted my arm. "Then it's settled. Next time you and Bev get together, I'll give her the painting for you. I have to go mingle. So great meeting you, Em. Is that okay? Calling you Em?"

The words stripped from my brain, I nodded like a brainless bat.

Her nickname brought me back to the present and thoughts of Price.

"See you in a bit," Sheila said before taking off.

"Want a cookie?" Bev called to me.

I really wanted to lie down, close my eyes, and dream of my mom. Instead, I took a PB&J cookie and a closer look at the paintings.

The back pocket of my jeans buzzed. Price wasn't one to give up easily.

Come on. I'm lonely.

He'd added a puppy emoji at the end, to which I replied:

You should get a puppy.

I should. Let's go tomorrow and pick one out. I'll adopt a lonely, abandoned pup.

He was relentless, I had to give him that.

I took off work tonight, so I'm working a double at the bar tomorrow.

So, let me take you tonight for some good food, and then we'll get the pup on Sunday. You need to eat.

Loneliness and wanting to get away from the ghost looming behind the damn coffee-cup painting won, and I shot off a quick text.

Tell me where to meet you.

Nope, send me your location. I'll come grab you in an Uber, and we'll go.

I knew there was zero sense in arguing, so I complied, and then went about hanging around the counter with Bev until he texted

Here.

Bev and I agreed to get coffee early the following week, and then she wanted to show me her dance studio. We said Tuesday or Wednesday, and I was out the door without a glance behind me.

Price flung the door to an Uber open and yelled, "Hey there!"

"Where's Johnny?" I slid into the back seat of the black sedan.

"Don't be mean."

"I'm not," I told him, pulling the door shut behind me. "I was honestly asking."

"I told him to take his wife out. They had a babysitter for their five-year-old."

The car stuttered in stop-and-go traffic; the driver seemingly knowing where to go. We jerked forward and came to a fast stop.

"Geez, I don't think I could ever drive here."

"I did when I first got here. Determined to do this my own way."

"I thought a limo picked you up and brought you to the Big Apple?"

When I referenced our conversation during our first dinner out, Price smiled.

"You remembered what I said. Well, another perk of being my dad's son is a sleek Tesla kept in the garage underneath my building. To get me out to the Hamptons, where, yes, my dad owns another place. Keep your judgy opinions to yourself. Anyway, refusing a ride from Johnny, I tried to take the Tesla to class one day. My patience for all the traffic here was nonexistent, so I didn't try again."

"Ha! I drove myself here and then sold my car when I got as far as Queens. I needed the money. It's been a month, and this is the first time I've thought about selling it, unloading all my stuff, and taking a cab to a three-star hotel."

People and cars whizzed by both of the passenger windows. The city was lit up like Christmas all around us, frenetic energy buzzing in the air.

"But I don't know how people keep up with this pace forever," I said to the window.

"Crazy. I'm still settling into it, and on the farm, we keep long hours."

"The thing is, I can't ever get that car back."

"You'll get a new car," Price said, running the tips of his fingers over my hand.

My eyes started to water about the damn car. "Jesus, this is the most inconvenient thing. I'm getting all teary over a car. With you. It's just that my dad got me that car. I guess I shoved everything about my dad to the back of my mind when I got here. I haven't even told him I sold it."

Price wove our fingers together and squeezed my hand. "You could always tell him that prick Robby sold it."

I couldn't help it. I burst out laughing. "Stop."

"Made you laugh, though."

I nodded and smiled through damp eyes.

The Uber came to a stop, and I saw we were in front of a big storefront.

"What's this?" I asked.

"Come on," Price said.

"Is this what you do on a Friday night? Shop for housewares?"

As he held the door open for me, I took him in. Worn jeans, hole in the right knee, and sneakers on his feet. His eyes matched his faded blue T-shirt. With his hair messy and framing his face, he certainly could have been a model or whatever. But he wasn't.

He turned toward me. "Come on. You can help me pick out a nightstand."

"Seriously?"

"No fucking way, pardon my language," he said while grabbing my hand.

He stopped for a second, looking around for something, and when he spotted an elevator, he pulled me that way.

"Should I be concerned?"

"Nope. All the chatty chicks in my class said the restaurant here is the place to go, so I figured we'd try it."

As we waited for the elevator, he explained. "I had Rudy, the doorman, call for me. Apparently, he can get reservations anywhere. Mrs. Flugel in the penthouse introduces him to all the right people on the phone, and he manages her reservations."

"Is that so? Has she been to my Bangladeshi place?"

Crap. As soon as I mentioned it, I remembered I hadn't showered and changed since serving lunch. "Ugh, look at me. I forgot I was in jeans and flip-flops. You think I can go in?"

"Stop it, you look great. This city's also weird with all the fancy dressing up, and for what? Just to eat?"

The elevator dinged, and the door opened to the most eclectic restaurant I'd ever seen. Mismatched chairs, funky glass chandeliers, potted plants lining the walls, and glass tables.

"I'm going to bring Mrs. Flugel out for lunch this week," Price told me as we waited for the hostess.

"Don't you dare."

"Oh, I never back down from a dare."

"Hi, can I help you?" A peppy redhead, wearing the shortest black shorts I'd ever seen and some sort of crop top, interrupted our moment.

"Reservation for Barnes," Price told her, only bothering to take his eyes away from me for a beat or two.

Yeah, I'm here with him.

"Right this way, Mr. Barnes," Little Miss Hot Shorts said, her tone a bit cooler this time.

I decided to enjoy myself. I'd never had the attention or passion of someone like Price, and I'll be damned if I wasn't going to savor it.

CHAPTER
FOURTEEN

Price

"Tell me, if you could buy one thing in this store, what would it be?"

We sat at the railing on an upper level, Emerson sipping a coffee while I enjoyed a bourbon on the rocks. The furniture store sprawled out below us was definitely the weirdest concept I'd seen in New York yet, but the food had been good. And Em seemed to be enjoying herself.

"Me? I don't think there's room in my apartment for anything from here."

"Come on, one thing. What's the point of eating here if you can't pick out something? You know what? It should be a like a Happy Meal. They should let everyone who orders an entrée take a souvenir home."

This made Emerson laugh, her chin tipped up, her hair spilling down her back. She'd had it in a messy bun when I first picked her up, but she'd quickly tugged it out, allowing it to hang loose in long dark waves. It was an inky mess like the lake at night, rippling with invitation, beckoning me to come closer. My hand itched to run through it, pull her next to me, and kiss her softly.

Emerson was like an after-dinner drink—you tasted her slowly, enjoyed every last morsel, and yearned for another long after you were finished. It was hard not to roll my own eyes at the cheesiness of my own thoughts, but they were what they were.

"Okay, I'll play," she said, jarring me from my daydreams. "I would take that armoire."

She pointed toward a distressed white cabinet, small drawers down one side, a cabinet running the length of the other. The paint was chipped in a perfect pattern because it had been manufactured to look that way. At home, we had plenty of pieces like that—except they were worn from actual use and making memories.

"That?" I pointed toward the piece on display.

"That. Sorry to disappoint. Did you think I'd pick that oversized bed with furry throws and pillows all over it?"

This time, it was my turn to laugh out loud. I couldn't help myself. "In your dreams," I told Emerson, but to be honest, I did hope she'd pick a bed, preferably with me in it.

Mentally slapping myself for my dickish thoughts, I asked, "Why? Why that armoire?"

"It's silly . . . but it looks like it's begging for memories, to be filled with a lifetime of good times, maybe a few sad moments thrown in. Don't get me wrong, I had a great childhood, and my dad did what he could. We didn't go to Disney World or the Grand Canyon. I didn't have big birthday parties or sleepovers with a bunch of girls doing makeup. We lived at the beach, and we'd fly kites or go go-karting. We'd eat crabs in the summer and makes s'mores over a campfire down by the shore."

"Sounds like you have some pretty damn good memories."

She gave me a small smile, but her eyes held that tinge of sadness I'd seen before. I could tell she wanted to know her mom, make memories with her, and fill that damn cabinet with pictures and mementos. I recognized it because I'd dreamed about meeting my dad for years, and now I had. And we weren't making any fucking memories.

"Huh. I've never been to Disney World either. Wasn't high on the list for my family. I've also never been to the Grand Canyon. Do you think it's scary being at the top? You know what? Don't answer. Let's just go there." I downed the rest of my bourbon and leaned back in my chair, watching her cheeks pink up.

"We just met. We can't go away together."

"Why not? I'm nice, safe . . . and I have a black Amex card," I teased, winking.

"I wasn't even allowed to spend the night with my high school boyfriend. Now I'm going to jet off to a different state, a different time zone, with a guy? My dad would freak."

"What about Robby?" I leaned forward, his name coming out with a small snarl. "Would he freak?"

After taking a long sip of her coffee, Emerson said, "About that. We're over. I guess it's good we never really started. Apparently, I'm an embarrassment to him. I guess you were right . . . he wasn't confused over me. It seems my not going to school is a deal breaker where he's concerned."

"Can't say I'm upset." I paused, knowing I had to be slightly more transparent. "Listen, I have to be honest with you—"

"Look, I'm sure you have someone else. I mean, why wouldn't you?" Refusing to look at me, Emerson traced patterns on the tablecloth with her finger.

"I don't. I thought I did. I don't want to lie. I had a life before being plucked out of it and dropped here. I worked, I dated a girl named Moira, and I had plans to make that my life for many years. Being here wasn't my choice, and I was mad in the beginning, but it's starting to look better. I do like my classes, and you. Moira and I, we had an arrangement to date other people. She's dating, I'm dating, and now—we've called things off altogether."

Emerson was still staring at the table, making it hard to read her.

"Look at me, say something," I said softly.

"Is that the truth?" She lifted her gaze, her eyes wide open and vulnerable.

"It is. Honestly, she didn't want me anymore. She said I'm never coming back from this adventure, and maybe she's right. Maybe I was fooling myself, thinking I'd go back. But I can't sit around and live off some other dude's money forever. Which is why we have to go see Mickey soon."

This got me a giggle, and I released a relieved breath.

Emerson eyed me over her coffee cup. "So, what are we? Dating?"

"Definitely," I said. "Want to get out of here?"

Biting her bottom lip, she stared at me with eyes the size of coasters.

"Not for that," I told her. "Let's just go walk and enjoy the night."

She nodded and I took her hand, leading her out into the summer night, the air heavy with humidity and promise. For the first time since my father rolled up to my house in that limo, I felt grateful for his generosity.

My phone rang on Tuesday as I was leaving class. The end of the summer term was near, and after our date on Friday, I'd spent the remainder of the weekend studying for a series of exams.

Em worked a double on Saturday and picked up a shift at the restaurant on Sunday, so she had to cancel our plans to get a dog. Which, admittedly, was a little nuts on my part.

But I was homesick, and a four-legged friend would definitely ease the ache.

"Hello," I said into the phone, walking down the street, knowing exactly who it was. *My father.*

"Price, how are you? How's school going?"

"Good."

"Look, I'm sorry that I haven't been around. I have some personal stuff going on, plus I'm selling off a business—"

"Look, you don't need to make excuses," I said, interrupting him. And I meant it.

Jamming the phone between my neck and shoulder, I resettled my baseball cap, shoving my hair underneath. It was a nervous habit, but hearing my dad's voice brought out all the anxiety in me. What did he really want from me?

"I need to explain more in person," he said. "I was thinking of coming into the city next week. I need to grab some files, and Monday is a dead day for me. Could we have dinner? Sit down so I can explain?"

"Sure."

It felt rude to say no, in light of all the money he was spending on me and my current lifestyle. My mom kept telling me to enjoy it, and honestly, I was now happy that I could spend time with Emerson, and share some of the privileges he gave me with her. But at the end of the day, I was used to working for my own money, supporting myself.

"I'll email you the time and place," he said.

"Okay."

Geez, he's not even going to swing by and see the place he pays for?

A woman called out to him in the background, and my dad said he had to go. The call was over. Clearly, all my dad was interested in was paying reparations. Being a part of my life was never part of his plan, and it certainly wasn't now.

Deciding to grab an espresso and call Emerson when I got home, I started to think about her mom. If she'd wanted to find her daughter, wouldn't she have?

People only do what they want or feel they should be doing, right?

CHAPTER
FIFTEEN

Emerson

I fell asleep talking to Price the night before. It felt like such a girlie thing to do, something I'd want to tell my mom about, but . . . I didn't have a mom.

It was now Wednesday, and I'd taken the day off to be with Bev and see her studio. She was teaching a noon class, and I was going to watch, and then we were going to go see her mom. I couldn't stop thinking, *Sheila wants me to take the painting.*

That thought was like an ever-present pounding in my head. Quite frankly, I hadn't a clue what I would do with the painting once it was mine.

All of a sudden, my gut clenched with fear. I should tell Bev the truth. She was my only real friend in New York City. Bev and her mom were being so kind to me—what if they decided to stop sharing information? My conscience told me I should be honest with them, but I couldn't risk it.

Making my way down the street after exiting the subway, I easily found Bev's dance studio and yanked on the heavy glass door.

"Yay! You made it." Bev was standing in the front by the counter.

"Told you I would." I winked and looked around. Every inch of wall space was covered in light pink satin slippers and awards, like *Best of New York, Best of Broadway, Tenth Annual Macy's Day Parade Attendee.*

Bev grabbed my hand. "My class starts soon. Let me get you situated."

We walked through a parent waiting area with a two-way mirror and into the studio where ten of the tiniest ballerinas all in pale-pink leotards and white tights sat waiting for Bev.

"Morning, ladies," she said to the miniature people.

They all smiled brightly, the world set in front of them.

"My good friend, Emerson, is here today to watch you perform."

"Hi, Emerson," they sang in unison.

"Shall we get started?"

The girls scrambled to their feet and hurried toward the bar.

Bev worked them through a series of footsteps, calling out different positions, and the girls responded to every command. Next, they made their way out to the middle of the floor and practiced their upcoming recital piece.

Their adoring moms were on the other side of the mirror, watching each step carefully, hanging on every twist, turn, and plié. I couldn't imagine a mother caring so damn much about another being, more than their own self, to want so much for another person, to fantasize about their future happiness. It seemed so foreign to me.

"Miss Bev, dance for us!" one of the tiny girls called out after they finished their class.

"My friend's here today. Next week."

There was a collective, "Aw, please?"

Bev blushed but didn't meet my eye as I said to her, "I can step out?"

Before I could stand up, a small ballerina was leaning on my knee, her bright eyes meeting mine.

"Tell Miss Bev to dance. She's so good."

I let out a big sigh. "Bev, I can't deny this one. Give us a twirl or two."

"Yay!" The girls all plopped down along the wall next to me.

"She has to change her shoes," one of the girls said to me.

A quick glance toward Bev confirmed their assumption.

She stepped out of what looked like dance moccasins and slipped into her ballet shoes. After lacing them up, she performed some sort of stretching and pointing with her feet.

Standing, Bev smoothed her lightweight skirt down and made her way to the music system. I'd never heard the music before, but it sounded like a combination of jazz and classical.

It didn't matter, though, because as soon as Bev started to move, the music became an afterthought. Seriously, she looked like a gazelle floating through the air, her feet lifting off the ground with ease, her low ponytail swishing behind her with every circle and turn, as if she were grace personified.

Applause rippled through the air as she finished. The small army of tiny ballerinas jumped up and swarmed around Bev, gushing over her performance.

When she released them and they ran out to meet their parents, Bev began straightening up the room.

"That was incredible," I told her. "You need to do more of that."

"I don't have the time. Wish I did. But the bakery, my mom . . ."

"Maybe I could help with the bakery?" The words burst out of my mouth on their own, as if they knew how desperate I was to be close to Sheila and my mom.

Bev shook her head. "I couldn't let you do that. You already work two jobs. Besides, it's not a high-paying position." She slung her bag over her shoulder and said, "Let's go."

I followed behind her, but I couldn't shake the idea of her giving up her dancing for her mom and the damn bakery. That wasn't her dream.

"Want to grab a coffee on our way?" Bev asked.

"Sure," I said, still deep in thought.

Walking into the coffee shop, ordering a latte, it all felt like a dream sequence. Our feet carried us several blocks, and then Bev motioned toward a small building with a stoop out front and a few steps that led to the door. There was a buzzer for guests, but no doorman—this wasn't a giant skyscraper like where Price lived. It was humble for New York, and it suited Bev and Sheila perfectly.

With her coffee in one hand, Bev used her key and then pushed the door open, ushering me inside. I followed her up three flights of stairs until we stopped in front of an apartment door.

"Come on," she said.

We traipsed inside, setting our bags inside the door. I followed Bev's lead and took my shoes off.

"Mom?" she called, making her way into the small kitchen to grab a banana.

"In here," Sheila called from down the narrow hallway.

We found her in her bedroom, sitting on top of her comforter, her feet in slippers, a plush robe tied tight at the waist, and a recipe book in her hands.

"Hi, ladies," she said.

"What are you doing, Mom?" Bev asked, eyeing the cookbook.

"I'm going to come in this week and try a few new cookie recipes."

"Mom." Bev sat at her feet. "No, you're not. We have enough cookies, and Fred does a fine job baking your recipes. You need to concentrate on getting better."

I felt like a peeping Tom in the doorway, watching someone else's life, smiling at their bickering and desperately wanting all that for myself.

"I need to get out of here, do something else other than lie around like a corpse. I'm not dead yet. Right, Emerson?" Sheila looked toward me.

"Um . . ."

"You don't have to answer that," Bev said, rescuing me. "She's worried about the bakery . . . worries it's going to fall apart."

Sheila shook her head. "This is New York, Bev, you know that. A new place could open up two doors away, and we'd be crushed. We need to spark some new reviews and interest with different recipes."

Walking toward the bed, I found my words with a certain courage I didn't know I had. "I was just telling Bev I could help at the bakery, and I love to cook. I could try baking. Why don't I come in and help with the new recipes?"

"See!" Sheila sat taller and eyed Bev. "And fresh faces, like Emerson."

"Of course you two gang up on me." Bev said it with a giggle, and she didn't seem mad.

"Look at this one," Sheila said as I sat down next to Bev. I wasn't sure whether it was appropriate or not, but it felt good, like being part of a family.

"Boyfriend cookies," Bev read. "Hmm, do they come with a guy?"

"Mmm, they look good, with or without a dude," I said, peeking over her shoulder.

"That's because you found yourself a dude within minutes of being here." Bev elbowed me while talking.

"I didn't find anyone," I said quickly, but my heart disagreed.

Bev scoffed. "Oh, please. I've seen you chatting and texting with Price on the phone, and I could feel the heat rolling off you."

Shelia tore her gaze away from her cookbook. "Who?"

"Price. Some guy Emerson met and then coincidently ran into again, and now it's a thing."

"Oh," Sheila said absently, staring back at the cookbook, but I could tell her mind wandered.

"You okay, Mom?" Bev asked, looking concerned.

"I'm fine, baby. I was just going through some ways in my mind . . . how we could personalize these boyfriend cookies. Make them unique to us. I was thinking of caramel chips."

"What if you added some liquor?" I asked, ever the bartender. "You could do a happy-hour collection."

Sheila's face brightened. "I hadn't thought of that, but it's great. We could do a whole line of cookies with liquors and serve them in the evenings."

"First, let's make the boyfriend cookie. Then we can start boozing it up," Bev said.

"Yes, Mother, dear. Whatever you say," Sheila joked back.

"I saw Bev dance today," I said, feeling like it was time to shift the focus to her. "Wow, I was blown away."

Sheila beamed. "She's pretty good, right?"

I nodded. "Incredible. I don't how she moves like that. I'd be in the hospital with a broken ankle."

"She's been full of grace since day one. I keep telling her to let me hire someone at the bakery, so she can go full time to school."

"Mom, enough." Bev shook her head, and some of her hair fell loose from her bun and shielded her face.

"Oh, I almost forgot why you came by. Let me get up," Sheila said while shooing us off the bed. After slipping out of bed, she padded off and opened a closet.

"Here!" She pulled out the matching painting to the one at the bakery, and my mouth watered.

My mom had touched this, painted this, and it was mine. It was the only thing I owned connecting me to my mom.

"I love it! You have no idea how happy this makes me." My hands trembled slightly when I took ownership of it.

"Enjoy it," Sheila said.

"Now you have to let me help at the bakery," I told Bev. "I can't just accept this and not pay you back in some way."

"You don't play fair," she grumbled at me, still smiling.

Bev was all bark and no bite like my dad, which reminded me. He didn't deserve my cold shoulder anymore.

I had to call Dad. Holding this painting made me ache for him in a way I never had before. He'd be furious I was here, clinging to the damn painting like it held meaning, but he'd still be happy for me. At least, I hoped he would.

My mom didn't deserve my respect. Dad did.

Yet, here I was, still searching for clues, for anything to bring me closer to her.

Holding back my emotions, I chatted more with Bev and Sheila, but all I could think about was getting this painting home and hanging it on the wall where I could look at it every day.

CHAPTER
SIXTEEN

Price

It's Sunday. You need a day off, and I need to run a few errands with you.

I texted Emerson super early Sunday morning, before my run. Most likely, she was still sleeping, so I didn't wait for her to answer.

Wearing my earbuds, I took to the pavement, winding my way toward the high line. The main streets were quiet, traffic at a minimum, and I could find my way there with little problem. Once I hit it, I ran all the way to the end and back up again.

My mind needed the exercise as much as my body. I'd been working overtime with studying, trying to make myself be upset over Moira, and counting the minutes until I saw Em.

My phone dinged as I huffed my way down my block.

I am off. I was going to sleep the day away.

Pick you up in 90.

You mean Johnny will pick me up.

Don't be such a know-it-all. I meant me.

Quickly, I hit the shower, changed into jeans, boots, and a ratty white T-shirt. I didn't need to be dressed up for where we were going. After stopping to consult with Rudy for a few minutes, I found myself unlocking the Tesla for only the second time since moving to the city. It was a far cry from my pickup truck. I felt like I was in a video game, not a damn car.

Following the GPS, I headed toward Emerson's place. For shock value, I didn't go up to the door, but rather texted her that I was here while double-parked outside.

As Emerson came out the door, she said, "What the . . ."

Leaving the car in park, I slipped around the front and opened the door for her. "Let's roll."

"We're not going to the Hamptons, are we? I have to work tomorrow."

"I wish, but no. I have too much studying to do, no can do."

She looked perfect in white jean cutoffs, her long legs stretched out on the floorboards, and a red tank top. Her hair was down, hiding her profile from me, but I guessed she was smiling.

"We are going somewhere fun, though," I told her. Angling the GPS toward me, I entered a new destination, and off we went.

"Did you ever have a boyfriend cookie?" she asked out of nowhere.

"Can't say that I have. Care to tell me more? Is that some sort of proposition?"

"Uh, no. Basically, they're like a kitchen-sink cookie. They have everything in them—mini candies, chocolate chips, nuts. They're made to be soft and gooey."

I gave her a grin. "You had me at soft and gooey."

"Come on." She punched my arm.

"Hey, don't hit the driver."

"Bev's mom is going to make them in her bakery. I was just wondering if some farm girl ever made them for you back home."

"Are you asking if someone loved me enough to bake me cookies?"

"Never mind. I'm being nosy. It's just you met Robby and were less than impressed. And I look stupid, the way I told you I was holding out for him, and fought with my dad over him."

She refused to turn her head, staring out the windshield.

Reaching over, I took her hand. "I don't think you're stupid. And, yes, I've had a few dozen cookies baked for me, but you know what? None of them were boyfriend cookies from the gutsiest, ballsiest, fun-nest—I know that's not a word, and I'm not some hick—cutest woman I know."

"I'm cute?"

"How 'bout gorgeous? Sexy?"

She shook her head. "Shush. Remember I grew up with a single dad? Compliments about my looks make me uncomfortable."

"How about, I bet you have a wicked arm in softball. Does that make you nervous?"

"I do, by the way."

"Of course."

"Wait? Did we just enter New Jersey?"

I nodded.

For the rest of the drive, we made casual conversation, talking about our favorite cookies. Me, plain old warm chocolate chip. Emerson, snickerdoodle or peanut butter.

"Where are we?" she finally asked.

"West Milford, New Jersey," I said, like it was an everyday drive for me.

"Oh, and now what?"

"We're going to turn right here." I flipped on the turn signal and drove down a gravel road.

"Sea Manor Kennels? Oh my God, you're getting a dog. Have you thought this through?"

"I have."

When we stopped in front of the farmhouse, I rushed around to open the door for Emerson.

The front door opened, and a middle-aged woman came out. "You must be Price. I'm Patty."

I gave her extended hand a small shake. "That's me. Yep, I am pumped. Thanks for holding the pup for me until I could get out here this weekend. Things get lonely in my apartment."

"He's a doll. Last one of the litter. And you are?" She looked at Emerson, her eyebrow raised, probably because I mentioned being lonely while having a hot-blooded female by my side.

"Emerson."

"Do you like dogs?"

"I do, but we don't live together." Emerson laughed while saying it, letting me off the hook. "He'll be responsible for all the house-breaking." She pointed at me.

Patty smiled. "Well, I can't help if you fall in love with this guy too."

"She means the dog," I said, unable to stop myself.

All I got from Emerson was an eye roll.

"This way," Patty said.

"You okay in flip-flops?" I asked Emerson as we walked toward a barn.

"I could live my whole life in flip-flops."

Another thing I couldn't help . . . I let Emerson go first, enjoying the view of her walking on a farm, wearing Daisy Dukes and flip-flops.

Yes, I let my mind wander, thinking about what she'd look like back home at my farm, with me, and I liked it. A lot.

Thank God, Patty and the puppy stole me from my runaway happily-ever-after thoughts.

CHAPTER
SEVENTEEN

Emerson

Inside the wooden building in a small pen, the tiniest ball of yellow fur was jumping around. Patty opened the gate and let the little guy walk over to Price, who was crouched down and waiting.

"Come here, little man," he said softly.

Clumsily, the puffball walked over to Price, already in love—because that's what Price did to all creatures.

"What kind of dog is he?" I asked.

"English Labrador," Patty said. "He'll grow to be about seventy-five, eighty pounds."

I looked at Price. "Can you have that big of a dog in your place?"

"Sure can."

And just like that, Price was nuzzling the puppy in one hand and pulling a wad of cash out of his pocket with the other.

Patty said her good-byes and handed Price a list of supplies. He glanced at it and said he'd already bought most of them the day before.

Once the pup had peed on the grass, Price clicked a small red collar around his neck, swung the car door open for me, set a blanket on my lap, and plopped the dog right on top of it. I was trying to resist falling in love with the animal, and now there was no way out of it.

"Tuck" slept on my lap all the way home, his puppy breath invading the car, and I was practically a proud mom.

"Who will take care of him when you're out at class?" I asked Price, stroking Tuck's fur.

"Rudy set me up with a dog walker. And you can visit anytime you want. Not because you have to do anything, just to see him."

My heart beat like a marching band in my chest. I'd never experienced anything like this with someone. It felt a lot like sharing a very special moment reserved for couples in love.

"Don't let your brain go into overdrive," Price said. "I see you overthinking it. Tuck's a damn cute pup, and you can feel free to visit him."

"Okay," was all I said.

"Good."

We drove back, both of us sneaking admiring glances at each other and Tuck.

Later, with Tuck asleep in his crate, a bottle of wine and empty cartons of Chinese food on the coffee table in front of us, a shiver ran through my body, despite me doing my best not to expose my anxiety.

I wasn't scared of Price. He'd never hurt me or push me to do something. My own insecurities and general lack of experience when it came to the prospect of having sex put the fear of God in me. Usually, I covered up my nerves with a hard candy-coated shell. But my shell was failing me tonight.

"Em, look at me." Price lightly tipped my face toward him. "Where'd you go?"

We were lying on the couch, me settled on top of him, between his legs. My head rested on his chest, my hair fanning out behind me, his hardness making itself known.

I didn't know what to do with all of these feelings, both physical and emotional. The whole scenario was daunting. It was like preparing to jump off a cliff without a parachute. My emotions, the blistering heat in my belly, and the pounding in my chest were enough to send me into cardiac arrest. I could hear my heartbeat whooshing in my ears.

"Em? Earth to Em, come back to me."

"Sorry, I spaced out." My words croaked out. I didn't—couldn't—look Price in the eyes.

We had kissed a lot over the last few weeks, but he hadn't touched me otherwise. We hadn't given ourselves a chance.

He shifted slightly, and as his knee bumped mine, he covered my knee with his palm and steadied it. "Don't be sorry. What's wrong? Talk to me, Em."

"It's just . . . usually, I think I'm such a badass. Thought I had everything figured out, but I don't know shit. And I guess I'm scared," I murmured into his chest, still refusing to make eye contact. Another chill ran through me, and Price pulled me closer. "I know I put on this act, and sometimes, I don't think you're falling for it. I know you're not, so why do you let me get away with it?"

His hand ran down my back and up again, working its way around my shoulder until his knuckles met my cheek. They grazed over my face as his warm gaze beat down on the top of my head, challenging me to look at him. His breathing was even—one breath in and another out—unlike mine. While his chest rose and fell in an easy rhythm, my breath whipsawed in and out, and my heart pounded like a wild beast. I tried to mimic him, syncing my breath to his.

"You don't have to be scared or know anything at all or have everything figured out. That's called being young, living life, figuring it out as you go, Em. You need to gain life experiences. Preferably with me by your side. That makes you a badass. When you decide to make mistakes alongside someone else. Showing your inexperience to the world and not being afraid to raise your hand and ask for help."

My frantic pulse slowed a little at his words. "Well, it's a bit different. You're older and have more experience. You know what you're doing."

"So? I'm still going to make mistakes in life."

"No, what I mean is . . . I've never been with anyone, and now I want to be with you, and I worry about it, now that it matters," I said softly. Then I whispered even softer, "What if I mess everything up?"

When an earthquake came from below me and a loud rumble erupted from Price's chest, I looked up to take in his huge smile. Price continued to laugh, his eyes squinting, his mouth wide.

"Is that what this is all about? Do you think I'm worried? I'm not. When you're ready, I'll be waiting, and it'll be magnificent. Until then, my fingers, my hand, my mouth, I want them everywhere . . . on you, in you. And when you're ready—and only when you're ready—all of me will be inside you. There's no pressure, Em."

"Is that why you always cut the evening short? You're giving me space? I don't want that."

Squeezing my eyes shut, I leaned my forehead into his shoulder in shame, his dirty words from before making me high. Not in a romantic or sweet way, but more raw and real. I wasn't sure if they should be doing what they were doing to me . . . making me hot and bothered, making me feel sensual and wanted.

"I don't want gentle, or for you to go easy on me." I pressed my face further into his chest, my words and breath painting his skin.

"Don't you dare hide from me." He gripped my hair and gently tugged my head back. "No shame here with me and you. Hear me? It's why I never bring it up. I figured you'd tell me when you wanted to, or I'd find out when it happened naturally. Until then, I'm fine. I'm a patient man, and I was waiting for the timing to be right for you. Got it?"

I stared at him, this strong man, hardened already at twenty-three from real manual labor, determined to make something of himself despite the shitstorm surrounding him. His words were so special in their own way, with his feelings evident in each one.

"Huh? I didn't hear you, Emmy? You hear me?"

"But I don't really know what I'm doing when it comes to all that. I was supposed to do the deed, and I didn't . . . and now I'm in so deep with you, and I don't know what I'm doing. I don't want to disappoint you."

"And thank fucking God for all of that."

His breath feathered over my neck as he pressed a line of kisses to my jaw and back to my clavicle. We lay cuddled on his couch, leftovers from our dinner growing cold on the coffee table. "We're in no rush. I'm not going anywhere. Christ, I'm stuck here another three years for school. You better not be leaving this city if I have to stay here."

His words tickled my skin. His lips weren't smooth like Robby's, who had been my only real kiss, but they felt better. Like something true and honest, and alive.

With my heart thumping, I said, "I'm not ready."

"That's good. Neither am I."

My lungs constricted. "Why? Is it me?"

"Did you not hear me?" His mouth took mine in a kiss.

A soft moan escaped my mouth. At least my lungs were working again.

"I said I'll wait however long you need." He broke away from my mouth and ran his fingers through my tangled hair. "There's a lot to keep us occupied in the meantime."

Which was what we did.

CHAPTER
EIGHTEEN

Price

With my classes over and fall semester not starting for a while yet, I found myself bored for the first time in forever. Emerson worked a godawful schedule, but I didn't begrudge her that. I had nothing but respect for hard work.

The plans for my father to come to the city and have dinner with me tonight were canceled. He texted me late last night, apologizing, and told me he'd be in touch to reschedule.

I'd just decided to take Tuck home for a few days and see my mom and Bruce when my phone rang. When I saw the caller ID, I didn't want to pick up, but did anyway.

"Hello?"

"Congratulations, Price. I see you finished with all As this summer. You're doing me proud. Are you enjoying some time off?"

"Actually, I was going to see my mom for a few days."

"Oh." My father sounded disappointed on the other end. Deflated.

"Do I need to ask your permission?"

"No need to be a hard-ass, son. I was simply going to see if you wanted to meet me in Philadelphia for a night. I wanted to make it up to you for not being able to come to the city today."

"Um, I could. Are you working?"

"No, I have a sick friend who's in the hospital here. I'm visiting."

"Well, are you sure?"

"Yes, I can only visit for a few minutes every day."

Seeing my dad wasn't at the top of my wish list, but if I told my mom, she'd say to go.

"I could drive there and then home," I said. "Were you thinking this week?"

"How's Thursday?"

"I'll make it work."

I'd have to run a lot of miles between now and then to work off my anxiety. No way I could show up to see my dad with all the tension our relationship gave me bottled up.

"Oh, I have a dog now. So I'll find a place to stay that allows him."

"How about a lady? You have a girlfriend, or are you still pining for the girl back home?"

"It's complicated. Yes and no." Honestly, what did he care?

"Bring your girlfriend too. Call me when you're here. I'll make a reservation. I want to see who my son likes."

He disconnected the call before I could debate it.

"I can't go to Philadelphia this week," Emerson told me. "I work a double on Thursday, and Friday night is my best night for tips at the bar. I need the money."

"Okay. I'd rather spend the weekend with you, though."

She was curled into my side on my couch Tuesday night. She'd come over to see Tuck, bringing him a bone and squeaky toy. I'd poured her a glass of wine, and we joked about how I shouldn't be serving her.

"I could get arrested, you know? Giving alcohol to a minor." My finger poked her side, a small ticklish spot right below her ribs.

"Stop!" She giggled and held her wine tighter.

"Who cares if you spill? Not my place, really."

"Don't be crass," she said. "That's not you."

"You mean the criminal in me, getting my girl tipsy on expensive vino instead of downing cheap alcohol out in the fields?"

"Is that what you used to do when you were a teenager?"

Her hair spread all over me, I ran the tips of my fingers through the ends of it. I'd thought Moira was it for me, but we'd never had an ease like this. Just chilling, chatting, doing nothing.

"We did. We'd steal liquor from our folks and haul it out to the middle of nowhere, which is basically all around us, and get wasted. We'd lie around the fields, looking at stars and waxing poetic. We were nothing but a bunch of nobodies—and still are."

"Yeah, yeah. Don't start with that. You are somebody."

"To you, I guess."

"To a lot of people, I'm sure."

That right there—the way she kept pumping me up—was doing a number on me.

Of course, Moira and I did that, but in the rearview, it didn't feel real. Like we were pretending.

"Hey, I'm off school a little while longer. Want to go to the beach next weekend?" I changed the subject, turning us toward something less about me and my insecurities. "You can show me where you grew up. I'll drive, and we can take Tuck."

"Oh, sure, my dad would love that. Fallen for another guy, let me just drag him home and throw it in his face."

"Well, I'm a better man. I can win him over. We'll do it G-rated and all that."

"I'll think about it."

We didn't talk much more. My mouth found hers, and we spent a long while kissing, my hand roaming down her back and up again. She tasted like peaches and sauvignon blanc. I wanted to drown in the flavor. She didn't ask if I'd be seeing any girls back home, and truthfully, I didn't want to see any but my mom.

"I should go home," Emerson finally said, breaking the moment.

I nodded. "Let me call Johnny to take us."

She stood. "No, let him be. Walk me outside, put me in a cab."

"I'm giving you the money."

She shrugged and started putting on her sandals.

"Hey, you okay?"

"Yeah, a little sad. I miss my dad. It's not that I don't want to see him. I just don't want him to go all judgy-judgy. And I need to find my mom. I'm close. Did you know Bev knows her? Or her mom?"

"What?" I stood up straight after hooking Tuck to his leash.

"It's a coincidence how it all happened, and I haven't told Bev yet."

"Em, you need to tell her. Even I know that."

"Later. Right now, I'm way too close. I have to get to meet my mom."

I took Emerson's hand, and we walked quietly to the elevator. Once we were downstairs, I pulled her close. "When I get back from visiting my family, we need to have dinner, and you can tell me how you figured this all out. You sure you're not a spy?"

This got me a laugh.

"I'm sure."

I handed her a crisp Benjamin, waved over a cab, and waited for her to get in. "I hate this. You could stay, or I could take you."

"It's fine," she said, sliding into the seat.

"Text me when you're home. And think about next weekend with your dad," I told her before shutting the door. I'd rather go with her, but Emerson needed to think she was independent. I could tell that was half the issue with her dad—asserting her independence.

It was the same with mine.

I walked Tuck around the block, watching his tiny bum shake and him tugging against the leash, taking my mind off my impending trip.

CHAPTER
NINETEEN

Emerson

The bar was crushed on Thursday night. I barely had a moment to look up from mixing drinks.

When I finally did, there was Bev dancing with the bunny. She stood behind him, shaking her hips, leaning out to the side so everyone could see her face.

She'd been here for a few hours, downing cosmos, letting loose. Her mom had told her she was coming back to work, and there was nothing Bev could do about it. Bev told me this over her first drink, sucking it back faster than I thought possible. Mostly, she was worried this would cause her mom to fall sick again. Even though she knew it wasn't connected.

"Woo-hoo, I want to take the bunny home with me," she said, bellying up to the bar.

I set a water in front of her, and she gulped it back without arguing.

"Maybe another night," I told her, eyeing the bunny moving on to a guy, who I was pretty sure was more his flavor.

"Are you done yet?" she asked.

Her hair flopped to the side, revealing her long neck and delicate hoop earrings. Even in a dark bar, surrounded by drunks, halfway to trashed herself, Bev was a flower, meant to be a dancer.

"Another hour. Do you want to crash at my place?"

"Yesss. And then we can have bagels in the morning?"

"Of course. And maybe I'll come to the bakery and help?"

"Sure. My mom'll be there, so that'll be good. I'll have anotherrr," she said, her words starting to slow and slur.

"Stick with the water, babe."

Bev frowned but didn't argue.

"Go dance some more, sweat it out."

"On my way," she said, already half off her stool.

I worked another hour, cleaned up with Randy, collected my tips, and decided on a cab, considering Bev's condition.

Back at my place, we both crawled under the covers, Bev's soft snores filling the room. Sleep escaped me, so I slipped out from the sheets, not that anything would wake Bev. With a cup of tea in hand, I sat on the windowsill and thought about what Price had said.

I had to tell Sheila and Bev. Tomorrow.

Endless scenarios ran through my mind, sleep evading me until the sun began to peek over the horizon. Lucky for me, Bev was fast asleep, and didn't even flinch when I crawled back into bed.

At noon the next day, we had bagels before making our way to the bakery.

"Swear I didn't embarrass myself?" Bev asked me over a strong coffee.

"You didn't. You were totally fine. Having fun, that's it."

"Ugh, my head hurts."

"Drink some more coffee."

"I need a cheeseburger with fries."

"Want to go get one? I'll take one for the team."

We were sitting in a hole-in-the-wall bagel joint in midtown on our way to the bakery, both of us in my jean cutoffs and tanks, Bev's clothes from the night before forgotten at my place.

"No can do. If I want to keep dancing and maybe, just maybe, go back to school, there are no cheeseburgers in my future. Last night was already enough of a no-no."

"You should go back to school. Your mom's coming back to work, and you shouldn't worry. Plus, maybe I can help her. Like I've said."

"How 'bout you go to school?" Bev eyed me above her disposable coffee cup.

"I will, once I find my mom."

"Are you any closer?"

I nodded, thinking I would wait to say something until we were all together, when I was rescued by the ding on my phone.

Heya stranger was all it said with a picture of Tuck.

Against my better judgment, I felt my mouth pull into a huge smile.

"What?" Bev asked, staring straight at my grin.

"Did you see Price's new puppy?" I showed Bev the phone.

"Aw, look at him. What are you waiting for? Answer the hottie back." She shoved the phone back at me.

"I usually wait a few to answer."

"Why? There's no stupid rules, and he's obviously missing you."

I didn't care to explain my nerves over his obvious wealth of experience versus mine, or the nagging need to make up with my dad . . . and how that might be impossible now. Rather, I picked up my phone and tapped away at a response, leaving Bev sitting there smug-faced.

All good here. Hanging with Bev. And going to bake.

Almost immediately, the phone dinged again.

Tell her.

"He's busy," I told Bev and tucked the phone away in my bag. "Let's go. I don't want to keep your mom waiting anymore."

"Fine," she mumbled.

"These are incredible." I shoved almost an entire cookie in my mouth. "This is the best part of baking. Sampling," I said to Sheila.

We'd made a batch of the boyfriend cookies, adding what could be different signature items to a few. My hair was up in a messy bun, my mouth full of warm cookie, and my heart heavy with the need to come clean.

"I like the ones with the white chocolate chips," Bev said, taking tiny tastes of various cookies.

"Me too," I mumbled around half of another cookie.

"Your sweet tooth is pretty impressive." Sheila stood at the sink, her spiky hair hidden underneath a pink-and-purple scarf.

"My dad's is pretty bad too. I guess he gave it to me. We had dessert almost every night after dinner. I'm sure the PTA moms would've been disgusted to find that out. God, it smells like heaven in here . . ." I took a whiff, accentuating the inhale. "Like crack," I joked.

"I was allowed one treat per week," Bev said. "Don't fall so hard for my mom."

"Not my fault. That was all your ballet instructor," Sheila told her. "I was just following orders, like a good mom."

"Whatever, it doesn't matter now. We're eating cookies after all. Now I can eat and eat. By the way, the coconut is yummy too." Bev leaned back against the counter, her hair slicked back in a low ponytail, only half a smile on her face.

"Give me some." I snatched a bite, walking closer to the one person who'd quickly become my friend.

We were standing side by side at the counter, a tray of cookies in front of us. I didn't know what having a sibling would actually feel like, but I'd always dreamed of having one. A great huge mystery to me, like a unicorn, but I wanted one, nonetheless.

"What about your mom?" Bev asked after swallowing, almost as if she was asking about the weather or what subway I took. "Do you wonder about that? Maybe she had a sweet tooth too."

The words came out of her mouth easily. Not because she was trying to hurt me, but rather she thought we were kindred spirits. Both with single parents, always wondering about the parent who left.

I shrugged, but I couldn't get rid of the awful feeling dogging me. Again, not her words, just the awful contradiction of my current situation. Surrounded by the sweet smell, sugary smiles, and presumed love all around me, and here I was lying to these women.

My dad had fucked up along the way, but he hadn't raised me to be a sneak. That's what got my ass to New York in the first place. I couldn't sneak around and sleep with Robby. I had to be forthcoming with my overly concerned single father. *Christ*, I was an absolute idiot.

Finally, my guilt got the best of me. I didn't want to come clean, but these were my friends, and I didn't want to lie to them. Lying was wrong—my dad had taught me that.

"Um, I should tell you both something."

"What, honey?"

When Sheila actually stopped what she was doing, giving me her full attention, I wanted to take a picture of her loving expression and keep it for later. Who knew when I would have it again? Maybe never.

"This is hard to say." I wrung my hands in front of me, wishing I could be mixing batter, anything to take my mind off what was about to unfold. I yanked my hair out of the bun and let a few loose strands fall forward, shielding my face, and hopefully my emotions. My eyes burned, and the shiny bakery floor before me turned blurry.

"This is a safe zone. We've been gal pals for almost all of Bev's life. You can say anything, right, sweetie?" Sheila looked to Bev for backup. "What happens at the bakery, stays at the bakery."

Although she said it, I wasn't sure she'd still feel that way after I came clean.

"That's the thing," I said. "For all my life, it's only been my dad and me. He didn't want me to look for or wonder about my mom, but I couldn't help myself. He tried to be enough, to be both my mom and dad, but no matter how much he sheltered me, my heart wondered. I'd lie in bed at night, dreaming of my mom. What she was doing, what she looked like. Did she miss me? Think about me? Don't get me wrong, he was great, and how I treated him this summer was bad. I was acting spoiled, like a big baby."

"That's only natural," Sheila said gently, not knowing what I was about to say.

"I kept a lot from him. I'd open the window blinds at night and look at the stars. I'd find an unusually bright one and pretend it was my mom looking out for me. I'd talk to her . . . not her," I said, grabbing at my forehead. "At a dumb star that couldn't hear me. I'd talk about my period or boys or the girls in my class, whatever was bothering me. It was never above a whisper, because I didn't want my dad to know I was doing it. Then things went shitty with my dad."

"It happens. Teenagers," Sheila murmured. "That's part of growing up. I hate to say it, but it's the truth, honey."

"Well, he and I had a big fight at the start of the summer, over a boy, and I kind of walked away. Ran away. Although he watched me do it. I decided to look for my mom here—because she's from New York. I blew a lot of cash, and honestly, I didn't know what I was doing. Just chasing after a name and not knowing much about her. It's didn't get me far, just broke. It was more like a wild goose chase. Anyway, then I walked into this bakery and struck gold. I didn't plan it, but it happened. And I couldn't help myself, I kept chasing my mom. And during that process, I fell in love with you two. It was wrong of me not to say anything—"

"What do you mean?" Bev turned to face me. "In this bakery? What does that have to do with your mom? You're not making sense."

"Let her talk," Sheila insisted, as if she knew what the next words out of my mouth were going to be.

"I mean, the painting. It was signed Paula Dubois. That's my mom. Or at least, that was her name when my dad knew her. So, I think it's my mom. She did like art, I heard. I was so shocked when I saw it, I had to stop myself from cheering. My mom! I couldn't believe it. And then you got to rambling, Bev, and we became fast friends, and it wasn't two-faced or spiteful, I swear! You're my only genuine friend . . . except I kept this tiny secret. I wanted to hear more about my mom. At the time, it felt innocent, like I found a friend and my mom all at once. Like God was finally on my side, sending me two amazing things at the same time."

Bev paced in front of us, her expression furious. "So you took advantage of my sick mom, took her painting, and what? You were going to suck every last piece of information from her, and then leave us? Doesn't sound like you really valued our friendship like you're saying." She clenched her fists and stopped in her tracks. "Well?"

"No. I swear. It all just happened. Price said I should tell you, which is why I am. He was right, even though this is gutting me."

"Who?" Sheila asked. "I'm sorry, I'm just trying to keep track of everyone involved."

"Price, her boyfriend or whatever. He's irrelevant." Bev's head swiveled back and forth between the two of us.

"Well—"

Before Sheila could finish her sentence, Bev cut in.

"He is, Mom. He means nothing. Just a stupid boy," Bev spat. "This is all stupid. Look, Emerson, I don't know what you hoped for. Some juicy gossip, a beautiful family reunion, to use me and my mom, or who the hell knows. But none of that is going to happen. What can I say?"

Glaring at me, Bev went on. "You and I are not friends. And your mom—if she is your mom—she's got a ton of problems. Starting and ending with swallowing anything that makes her feel good. Drugs, alcohol, whatever. She can't even take care of herself, let alone you. You should be happy she's not in your life. Look at my mom, her best friend, suffering with cancer, and you'd think Paula would be here? Nope. That's Paula, the famous Paula Dubois you're looking for. Selfish to the core."

Sheila held up a hand. "I don't think you're being very kind, Bev. Stop." Her eyes glistened with unshed tears, but she didn't make her way toward me. She placed her hands over her cheeks, and her chest rose and fell with heavy breaths. "Oh God, you're Paula's daughter. I remember when she had you."

"I'm being more than kind, Mom. We don't need someone to use us for Paula." Bev continued to glare at me, but her mom ignored her.

"You look a lot like your dad. I've only seen a picture, one picture, a long time ago." Sheila sat on a kitchen stool and caught her breath. "Your mom had such a major crush on him. She loved him, or thought she did, but her parents wouldn't have any part of it. And then she ended up pregnant. They were irate, sent her to some spa place for the duration, kept her out of the Upper East's eye. At first, she refused to put you up for adoption. She came home to deliver you in New York, demanding her parents accept you. Only a few days later, she said she couldn't do it. I had Bev at that point, and couldn't do much for her."

Biting my lower lip, I thought about what she'd just said. "So, I'm the reason for all of her problems?"

Sheila shook her head. "No. She'd dabbled for a while in drugs. I think the only time she'd been under control was the month she'd stayed with your dad, and then while she was pregnant with you. After that, it was a brutal spiral. She'd do well and then not so well. For a while, she held it together. Was teaching and painting. Then she got married to someone else, but he was a man of few words and a lot of money. She blew through a big chunk of his cash, and he ended up walking out."

I don't know why I cared, but I asked, "Didn't anyone try to help her?"

"For real?" Bev glared daggers at me. "I spent my childhood watching my mom try to help her. When that dickhead husband of hers got smart, she really fell apart and stopped talking to anyone. Been 'on leave' ever since." She used air quotes, her fingers slashing the air.

Sweat beaded along my lip and behind my neck. This wasn't what I wanted for anyone. For me, my mom, or Bev and Sheila. "You acted like she was so nice when I asked about the painting."

"Because *my mom* always insisted we don't tell tales or stories about others' hardships. Now that it's your reality, I don't give a crap. God, I thought you were going to be my friend." She slammed her fist onto the counter. "Now you got what you really came for. Now you have the awful truth."

Sheila stepped toward me. "Paula always regretted leaving you, but she wasn't in the right way to find you, do you get that? I didn't encourage her to keep you, and maybe that was wrong, but she was a mess. And no one wanted to hand that over to you."

Bev scoffed. "So, Paula suffered? And you feel guilty about it? Mom, let Emerson be. She asked for this. She had a good dad, a good life, love, and none of this was her burden." Bev turned to me, her face pinched. "I want you to go, Emerson. Leave. Just go. I can't do this. I've had to give up everything important in my life, and this is one more thing."

I didn't argue or plead my case. Without another word, I turned and left. After all, Bev asked me to.

Sheila called after me, "Emerson! Wait."

The pull of her daughter was stronger than me, and Sheila didn't chase me. Was I surprised?

Not one bit.

I ran with my tail between my legs, all the way back to my apartment . . . and picked up the phone.

CHAPTER
TWENTY

Emerson

"Dad!" The second the call connected, I began to sob. I didn't even wait for him to say hello.

"Emerson, what's wrong?" Immediately, he went into Dad Rescue Mode. That's why I called him. When I wanted something fixed, I ran to my dad. He'd been my constant.

"Did you know?" My heart pounded at a furious pace while I waited for him to answer, afraid of what he might say. Would I feel differently about him if he had?

I'd fallen on my bed in my shitty apartment, in a heap of dirty clothes and tears, missing my bedroom at home for the first time since coming to New York.

"Know what? Robby said you guys broke up. Is that what has you upset? Baby, your heart will be broken a million times before you settle down. It should be . . . that's why I didn't want you to give everything to him."

His voice was steady, just like always. My dad was my rock. In light of recent information, I wondered what would have become of me if he hadn't kept me from making that huge mistake.

"Not Robby. I don't care about him." I pushed my head back into the pillow and cried hard.

"Em, you're worrying me. Tell me what's wrong. I'm not mad at you. I love you. Nothing could make me stay mad at you, I swear. I've been giving you space because that's what you needed. I trust you. Look what an independent woman you're growing into—"

"I found her."

"Who?"

"Paula, Dad. My mom."

"Christ, you saw her? Jeez, I wish I'd stopped you from this adventure."

"No," I whispered. "I didn't see her."

"All I ever wanted was for you to be happy, content, feel like you had a sweet life despite the shit circumstances. I knew finding her would be bad news."

"I randomly met this girl, and it turned out her mom had been friends with Paula. It was like finding the most perfect shell on the beach. I couldn't believe my luck."

I told my dad the rest of the story, not leaving out any detail, and he listened. He didn't interrupt or pass judgment.

When I was done, I asked, "That's why I have to ask . . . did you know?"

A long beat of silence passed, and then he said, "Paps did, not long before he died. He sent a detective to look for her. Found her high on Lord only knows what, out of her mind in some ritzy penthouse. Paps took the information to be an omen. You were better with us. We decided to keep you away from all of that. I'm sorry if it was wrong. You were loved. More than loved. Know that, Em. We tried to love you more than enough."

All the words stuck in my throat, I sobbed.

"Em, do you want to come home?"

"I don't know, Dad. I need time to think. Bev's my friend, and now I ruined everything with the only good friend I made. She's dismissed me. Plus, there's this guy . . . and maybe my mom is somewhere out there needing help, needing to know I grew up fine. Maybe that would help her . . . I just don't know. I'm confused."

It was a hard thing to admit, being confused, but it slipped out. Maybe because my dad was the only person who ever listened to me. Destined for heartbreak, I hadn't given up the ghost in finding Paula. What the hell was wrong with me?

"Don't torture yourself, sweetie. Your mom may be too far gone, and that's not on you," my dad said. "You can't help a person who doesn't want help. And it sounds to me like your friend told you, Paula doesn't want any help. That's not on you, or me. Look, Em, I did the best I could. Maybe it wasn't always the best or the way I should have done shit, but I'm just a guy with a daughter he loves to pieces."

"I'll let you know. 'Kay? That's the best I can do."

"Emerson, this is your home. Come anytime. Call me anytime. I love you, do you hear me? No matter what, I love you. It's always been you and me, honey. Please don't make yourself sick over this."

His worry for me was evident in his cracked voice. Yet I couldn't make myself stop this search.

"Love you," I said quickly and hung up.

Not sure how long I lay there, wondering why my dad's love for me wasn't enough. Why did I consider myself the only person who could really save my mom?

So there I lay, like a wealthy woman on TV eating bonbons, long enough for the sun to set and rise again. No school for me yet, since I hadn't gotten any clarity on anything since I left home.

Price took a seat at the bar on Saturday night. "Hey there, stranger."

"What are you doing here?"

"Getting a beer," he said, raising an eyebrow. "Am I not welcome? Someone else here caught your eye?" He smiled and pretended to look around the bar.

"Ha, no. You said you were going home after seeing your dad. Everything okay?"

"Well, good to know you were listening."

"Hey, I'm a bartender. I listen. It's what gets me the big bucks," I joked, but I could see something was off.

There was a tiny furrow between Price's eyes, a little divot of worry. His smile wasn't fooling me. I'd grown up around men, and I knew when they were trying to cover up their feelings.

"I was supposed to head there this morning," he said, not meeting my eyes. "But I changed my mind."

"Is that so?" I filled a chilled pint glass with the latest beer on tap and set it in front of him, not wanting to admit how happy I was to see him. A certain calm rushed over me, in a way I'd never experienced before.

"You sounded sad when I texted last night." He shoved his hand through his hair, and I noticed another small worry line in his forehead. It made me think of my dad, about someone caring about me, for me.

"I'm not sure how someone sounds like anything in a text . . ."

"Hush." He took a swig of beer before continuing. "You know what I mean. You were clipped and sounded down. Not your usual snarky self."

"Shit," I whispered, grabbing a rag to wipe the bar. Idle hands were the enemy when in uncharted territory. "So, it was me? I made you cancel your trip home? Your mom will hate me." How did he turn this around and make it about me? What was with men and their need to fix everything?

"Nah. It was a crap time with my dad. He was distracted, and basically, I was an afterthought, just like always with him. He was busy with an old friend who is sick or some shit. We had dinner Thursday night, and then I sat around all day Friday, waiting for him."

"But you had Tuck. That's a bright spot."

"It is. In fact, he misses you. Why don't you come back with me tonight when you're done?"

"Oh, I see you trying to get in my pants, using your dog."

This got me a big chuckle. The line in his forehead smoothed out, making my heart pound in relief. I hadn't known that was possible, a heart beating because of someone else's. I'd thought it was something made up in the movies.

"Em, what will I do with you? Here I am, wanting to cry in the beer only you and you alone poured, and you make me laugh. That's why I came to your bar, and nowhere else."

"I'm sorry." I smiled through the apology.

The smell of beer all around us, my body sticky from working—it was like a scene from a romance movie. *Not.*

"Don't be. I was feeling like shit, and now I'm not. You made me feel better already. I love my mom, but if I went there feeling low, she'd know in a heartbeat. And then she'd draw out every bit of my feelings, and analyze and dissect them, wanting to make me feel better. She'd make me feel worse without trying to, but still. Now I'm laughing. You take me as I am."

"I'm glad I could provide that service. Although, I wouldn't know what it's like to have a mom dissect me. Maybe it's fun."

"Believe me, it's not all it's cracked up to be. Go on, work, and then come home with me. Just to hang, scout's honor," he said, lifting two fingers. "We'll have fun, maybe make s'mores over my stove?"

"Okay, boss, but one quick thing . . . I'm off tomorrow. I thought you'd be away, so I was planning on cleaning my apartment and washing my hair. You know, big stuff."

"Well, now you're all mine. Go work."

True to his word, Price sat at the end of the bar watching a baseball game on TV until I was done. He didn't bug me or try to take me away from the task at hand. I didn't know devotion, but he certainly seemed full of it.

CHAPTER
TWENTY-ONE

Price

Once Emerson's shift ended, I took her hand in mine and walked her toward the car. Johnny had driven me out and said he didn't mind waiting.

"Poor Johnny," Em said. "It's so late."

"I did a public service. No joke, I think he relishes the time alone, watching a movie on his iPad while waiting. I'm sure his life at home is hectic."

"Shhh," she whispered, tucked into my side, watching Johnny run around to get the door for her.

"Where to, boss man?" Johnny asked me.

"Cut the crap," I said while laughing.

He gave me a big grin. "It's just too easy to get you."

"Yeah, yeah. We're going to my place."

"No problem," he said, and headed back to the driver's side.

Settled in the back seat, I threw my arm around Emerson and pulled her close. "Now, this is good, right?"

"Oh no!"

"What?"

"Tuck! You left him for so long tonight . . . because of me."

I shook my head and chuckled at what I was about to admit. "My building is full service. Had the nighttime guy go up and give him a potty break."

"Oh."

"Fuck me. If anyone back home heard me say that out loud, I'd be the joke of the town."

"Your secret's safe with me." Leaning her head on my shoulder, Emerson closed her eyes, and we rode in silence.

When we pulled up in front of my building, I jostled her gently. "We're here."

Watching her wipe her eyes with the back of her hand, I swallowed my hunger. I liked this chick—young lady, whatever—in ways I hadn't believed really existed.

"Come on." I took her hand and walked her in the front door and to the elevator. Up we went, my lips pressed to hers, until I broke free for a second and mumbled, "My mom's probably pissed I didn't come home, but this made it worth it."

Upstairs, Emerson asked if she could take a shower.

"Sure. Why don't I take Tuck out while you do that."

Of course, I would have rather joined her, but there was no sense in pushing. The time would come.

"Okay," she said quietly, and padded off toward the master bathroom.

Another lump of hunger, not for food, went down my throat. I was doing my best to stay in my lane. There was no rush, no reason to pressure her. But I wanted this woman.

To say I wasn't prepared for the sight in front of me when I walked back in with the dog would be an absolute understatement.

Right there, on my couch, Emerson sat, her hair hanging in wet strands, her long legs stretched out from beneath the towel that wasn't doing a good job covering her up. Her tits were loosely covered—it would only take one tug to free them.

"Hey," she said. "Your couch is like a cloud."

As soon as he was off his leash, Tuck ran and jumped up next to her.

"See?" she said with a grin. "Tuck agrees."

"I'm pretty sure he thinks you're like a cloud." I sat next to her. "In fact, I agree."

Sliding a loose wet strand behind her ear, I ran my lips down her cheek from earlobe to chin, her skin like a cool pillowcase on a hot night to my burning lips.

"Em," I murmured against her lips. "You're so beautiful."

"Thanks for rescuing me," she whispered back.

"You rescued yourself." My hand wound under her hair, my palm finding the nape of her neck, and I brought her closer. Her left thigh against my right, her front now flush with mine. I was dying to lay her down and be on top of her.

"No one's ever been there for me like you."

"We have a connection," I told her. "I like it . . . and I really like you." We kissed again, our mouths finishing the conversation.

When her fingers slipped under the hem of my T-shirt, goose bumps spread over my skin, and if I was being honest, my patience was disintegrating.

"Take me to bed," she said, her soft hand drawing figure eights on my back.

"Emerson, we don't have to rush."

"I want you to. Come on."

Pulling out of my arms, she rose on bare feet and started walking toward the bedroom. I followed. Inside my domain, she turned and dropped the towel.

"It has to mean something," I told her, struggling to breathe. And I meant it. "I don't want it to be revenge sex against your dad or your douche ex."

We stood so close, her breath ghosting my face, her chest rising and falling. She was so beautiful, and I wanted her so badly, but I wanted to be sure.

"I don't want to only be a distraction to your pain."

She shook her head. "It's none of that. None. It means maybe more than you know."

With a quick swipe of her hand, she removed my shirt . . . and any resolve I was holding on to.

Gently backing her into the bed, I spread her out in front of me, and shoved out of my cargos. Flip-flops, boxers, shorts all deposited in a heap, I lay down next to her and kissed her. It was agonizing to take it slow, but I did my best, my palm gently moving over the side of her breast and back up again.

She pushed into my hand, and her legs twisted with mine. Her heat met my thigh and she moved, trying to create friction. My lips found her nipple, and my finger found its way to her heat. She was so hot, burning for me, and it was a major turn-on.

Quiet whimpers made their way from her mouth until she was spent and ready for all of me. She fumbled with my length, but it didn't take long for her to learn how to caress me, just hard enough, the right speed, and then I grabbed her hand, stopping her.

Reaching toward the nightstand, I grabbed a condom. My fingers struggled to rip it open. Sometimes, nerves even got the best of us dudes. After it was on, I took Emerson's lips again in a kiss.

"You sure?" I asked, needing to confirm that this was what she wanted.

She nodded, and then I did something I hadn't done since I was fifteen years old. I went slow, not pushing in too hard, too rough, too quickly . . . until she squirmed and said, "I'm ready, please."

Once I was inside her, I ran my fingers down Emerson's arm, looking into her eyes. "Okay?" It came out gentle, my own resolve warring inside me. *Go fast, not too fast, claim this woman.*

"Yes. Move, please."

She didn't have to ask again. I moved in and out, closing my eyes for a moment, savoring each stroke. My past was nothing but behind me, my future somewhat clear.

It might have been eight years since I took someone's cherry, but it didn't mean I could hold on for long. Together, we hit a crescendo and . . . *wow* . . . I didn't even know what happened, or that it could happen like that.

"Let's go see your dad. Come on, it'll be fun," I said over coffee and pancakes the next morning.

Emerson sat across from me in one of my T-shirts, the left side falling off her shoulder, exposing her creamy skin and the length of her neck. Resisting the urge to run my tongue there, I took a sip of coffee instead.

"This again?"

"I've never been to the beach. Come on."

"I can't believe that. Wait, do you know how to swim?"

"Yes, I do, missy." I reached across the table and pinched her cheek.

She promptly stuck her tongue out at me and forked a bite of blueberry pancakes off her plate. "I'll say this, you've been holding out on me. These are good."

"My mom's recipe," I told her, trying to keep from getting emotional.

I missed my mom, and I was certain she saw through my lame excuse when I didn't visit her this weekend. *Homework*, I'd said. She knew me better than to fall for that, especially since the summer session was over and fall hadn't yet begun, but she let it go.

"It's crazy good," Emerson said. "Why don't we go there? And then I'll think about going to my dad's another time."

"It's August, and hot as hell. Let's go to the beach, and then we can go to my mom's in the fall."

The meaning of my statement hung in the air like the humidity outside. I was making long-term plans. Fall was only a month away, but I could see the surprise in Emerson's wide eyes.

"Em, you gave me something special last night. Now, don't go taking my man card for saying this." I took her hand in mine. "But this isn't some *hit it and quit it* thing, okay?"

Her knee bounced quickly under the table; I could feel her heel tapping on the floor.

"Also, I could make you better pancakes with the blueberries there . . ."

She swallowed, and I could practically see the thoughts ripple through her mind, the expression on her face going from shock to surprise to something softer.

"You just want me to make up with my dad," she said, changing the subject.

"I do."

"You left Philly mad at *your* dad."

"Different story. Feel me? Your dad's been with you since day one. Come on . . . he may not like the idea of me, but he'll warm up to me. And we'll bring Tuck. No one can resist the blond bombshell of a dog."

Emerson frowned. "I'll think about it, okay? Will that get you to be quiet? I'll call him later and see what he says."

"My lips are sealed. Now, what do you want to do today?"

Setting her fork down, she took a deep breath. "I was going to see if I could get a last-known address for my mom. I planned to go see Bev's mom while Bev is at her dance class. I know I shouldn't, that I should let it go, but I can't." She rambled, closing her eyes.

"Hey, can I say something?"

"Can I stop you?" A half smile ghosted across her lips.

"Bev meant, *means*, a lot to you. Why don't you try to see her too? Make a peace offering. Fall on your sword. Whatever type of words of wisdom they spout in those self-help books like *Friendship for Dummies*."

"I want to. Maybe I can ask Sheila—her mom—the best strategy, and get Paula's address while I'm there. Would you . . ." Emerson shook her head. "Never mind."

"Would I go with you? Yep. Then we'll go to the zoo. Nothing makes you feel better than the zoo. Done."

We finished eating over small talk until Tuck trotted over, carrying his leash in his mouth and running in circles. Deciding he wanted a walk, we obliged before going back to Em's for fresh clothes and to visit Sheila.

I wasn't sure it was a great idea, but I couldn't say no to Emerson . . . *until I could.*

CHAPTER
TWENTY-TWO

Emerson

"One sec," I called from behind my bathroom door.

"No rush," Price hollered back.

That was good because I was staring at myself in the bathroom mirror, wondering if I looked different. Like I wasn't a virgin.

It was another one of those moments where I wished for my mom, someone to confide in or who could tell me I looked like the same damn woman.

Young woman, obviously, but woman all the same. My heart rate sped up when I thought about what I did. What *we* did.

I'd known Robby most of my life, and I couldn't come up with one decent reason why I should have shared this moment with him.

Smoothing my palm over my neck and down my chest, I closed my eyes and remembered the exact moment Price was fully inside me. It had stung, but then felt more than right. Like we belonged. I wondered if it was normal to feel that way.

Again, I needed a mom.

This made me open my eyes again and get moving. After slipping on some clean clothes, combing my hair, and adding a touch of makeup, I was ready.

"Let's do this," I told Price, who was sitting on the edge of my bed with his phone in his hand.

"Everything okay?"

He nodded. "Yeah, my dad, apologizing, saying he wants to come here in a few weeks. Same shit, different day." He took my hand. "Are you sure you want to go see Sheila?"

I nodded.

Johnny picked us up in front of the building, and we settled quietly in the back seat. It was obvious I needed time to think, and Price was giving it to me.

When we arrived in front of Sheila and Bev's building, I felt bad, knowing it was sneaky to come when Bev was teaching dance, but I couldn't help it. I asked Price to wait in the car.

"I need to do this on my own," I said.

Darting to the door, I buzzed Sheila, who let me in the building and didn't seem surprised to see me when she opened her apartment door and asked me in.

"Emerson, I'm glad you came. Sit down," she said, patting the chair next to her.

"I want to say, I really love Bev. This truly was coincidence. God works in weird ways."

"You could say that," she said, and I didn't really know what she was getting at.

"I wish she and I could make up. I hope we do," I told her.

"You will. Bev can't keep a grudge long. She's like me. I mean, if your mom walked through this door right now, we'd pick up where we left off. No joke."

Sheila's eyes watered a bit, and I took in how weak she looked. No scarf today, only her buzzed hair.

I nodded, not knowing what to say.

Sheila went on. "Your mom isn't a bad person. I'm sure you feel differently, but I promise you she's not."

I leaned forward, not wanting to miss a syllable of what she was saying.

"Paula, from the outside, looked like she had a good life. Gorgeous, always the best clothes, money, freedom. But her dad was tough. Had a string of lovers, and her mom couldn't leave. She was bound by money. She would have none if she left, and she placed more importance on the money. Anyway, Paula looked at your dad as a chance to break free from it all, but things didn't work out that way. Then she met the man she married, and in the end, his money won out with her too. She'd always had an addictive personality, but after she left you, it got worse. She couldn't stand herself."

"But I—"

"I don't want you to confuse this as being your fault. It's not. You were a baby. That was her choice to let you go without anything. But she went downhill after she left you, until she got married. Then she cleaned up for a while . . . but only a while."

"Look, I don't care. I want to see her." I stood and paced. "Price . . . he came with me. He's waiting outside."

"Price?" Sheila asked.

"My friend. Boyfriend, I guess. Remember, Bev told you?"

"Oh, right," she said, waving off her confusion, but it felt like something more. I didn't know.

"I want to see my mom. Do you know where she lives?"

"I understand what you're asking, but I don't know. She's been MIA. For a while, she was living across from the park, right near Columbus Circle, but she hasn't been there in a while."

"Can you try to find out? I know I shouldn't burden you. And I'm sure Bev will be pissed, but you're my only chance."

Sheila nodded and closed her eyes. "I will for you. But you need to go talk to Bev. Later this week. Make amends. She has a lot on her plate with me, and she truly looked at you like a good friend. So, go to the bakery and hash this out, okay?"

"Yes. And thank you. So much."

"I'll call you, okay? And I will act like I don't know a thing when it comes to Bev. She needs a friend, and so do you. Remember that."

Price was waiting outside the car, his ass leaning into the door, and walked my way as soon as he saw me come out.

"It go okay?" he asked, wrapping an arm around me.

"Yeah, I think so. She's going to get me an address. But she wants me to make amends with Bev."

He opened the door for me to slide in as Johnny waited in the driver's seat.

"It's not going to be easy," I said, the back of my bare legs sticking on the leather as I slid inside the car.

"Nothing worth it is easy, right?"

"Is that right?"

"Well, being with you is . . . so, maybe I'm wrong."

He kissed me, and off we went.

"What now?" I asked.

"You'll see."

Johnny pulled up in front of Price's building, but instead of going inside, Price tugged me out of the car, took my hand, and crossed the street.

"Tuck?"

"He's with the dog walker. Come on," he said, entering Central Park.

I'd been in New York for a couple of months, but I hadn't even ventured inside the park.

"Pretzel or hot dog?" Price asked, nodding toward some street vendors.

"Pretzel."

"Done."

We jumped into line for a pretzel, and after Price paid for two of them, we walked and munched.

"They say it's the water that makes them so good," he said. "New York water . . . for both the pretzels and the dogs."

"Ha! I guess so."

"Same with the bagels."

"There's nothing like the bagels here," I said. "At the beach, people used to talk about the bagels from New York, and I thought they were kidding. Or exaggerating."

"Nope. They're pretty fucking good. Though, I miss some stuff from home. It was fresher or some shit," he said, looking wistful.

"You should've gone home."

Price shook his head. "Nah, it's all good. I'm just thinking out loud."

"Oh yeah, about what?" I tossed my pretzel wrapper in the garbage, tucked my hair behind my ear, and looked up at the man who was stealing my heart.

"I was thinking how I could bring a piece of home to the city."

"Um, I'm pretty sure somewhere along the way, you said you didn't like it here."

"It's growing on me," he said before swooping me up in one huge lift and tossing me over his shoulder.

"Put me down! I just ate," I said, but who was I kidding? I would have stayed.

When he put me down, I asked him, "So, what could you do?"

"I don't know. My final for my econ class got me thinking about some sort of urban-garden-type restaurant. It's been done before, but I could do it better. Make it down-home, authentic."

"Sounds so cool. You said the same kind of thing this morning when we were eating pancakes. You should look into it. Make some plans."

"We'll see. Right now, I'm living on borrowed money."

"The zoo," I said, seeing the sign as we approached. "Oh, I've never been."

"Come on."

As soon as we went through the gate, I squeezed Price's hand. "Thanks, this is fun."

"We didn't even see anything yet," he said with a quizzical look.

"I'm telling you now because I know it will be awesome."

Right there under the tree at the zoo entrance, Price kissed me. He kissed me hard first, close mouthed, and then soft, not letting up. I didn't want him to stop.

"I like you, Emmy B, and don't you forget it," he finally abandoned my lips to say.

"You're not so bad yourself."

"Come on, let's see some penguins."

CHAPTER
TWENTY-THREE

Price

"Let's go somewhere, get away from all this bullshit. It'll be fun," I said, Emerson's feet up on my lap as we chilled out on the couch.

It was Thursday, and the first time I'd seen her since the zoo. She'd spent most of her free time over the last few days dealing with her obnoxious boss at the restaurant, and trying to find a moment alone with Bev. Every time she went into the bakery, Bev busied herself in the back.

Emerson sat up and stared into my eyes. "You're such a softie. You want me to make up with my dad, don't you?"

"I do, but I also want to go in the ocean."

"Whatever . . . I guess we could. I'm not on the schedule for the bar this weekend, and I don't have the restaurant gig anymore. What a jerk. Can you believe it?"

"That he kicked you to the curb for a relative? Yes. It's not like the place was winning best place to work in the U.S. of A. anytime soon."

"Hardy-har. I made good money. I may not cover my rent now."

Not sure where it came from, but "You could move in here" just dropped out of my mouth.

Emerson gaped at me. "Stop. You're crazy. We just met."

"Think about it, and also about going home tomorrow. I'd like to see you in a bikini."

"Tell my dad that, tough guy."

"Well, I was going to be covert . . . just eye you up on the sly, and sneak into your room at night."

"Shit, there's my phone," she said, interrupting me. "Let me see if it's Bev."

I didn't mind. Her ass was on my couch, and this whole thing was really killing her.

"It is," she said, popping up to pace my living room.

Okay, my dad's living room.

I needed my own place. This joint was too beige. Too fancy. Extra as fuck. I couldn't move Emerson in . . . it wasn't even mine.

"She said she's sorry to be avoiding me, and she asked her mom, and her mom said there was no reason to be mad at me. This is great news, right? She's lucky to have a mom like that, so open and understanding."

"See? I told you. It's going to work out."

I thought back to my own friendships and relationships, and wondered when I became the least bit qualified to give advice. Basically, I had my beer-drinking buddies and Moira—who'd ended anything we had—and now I didn't give a single fuck. I guess she didn't really mean much to me. In a short time, Emerson had come to mean everything.

"Oh, she just asked if we could do coffee on Monday night!" Emerson was walking around the cream-colored carpet, phone in hand, smiling.

"You look like one of the penguins at the zoo, hopping around," I teased her.

She plopped in my lap. "Shhh."

"Kiss me and I will."

She did. Her mouth met mine, our lips a frenzy of pent-up hunger for each other, until her phone buzzed again.

Squeezing her ass, I told her to get it.

"It's Bev! We're on for coffee. You know what? Maybe now that I don't have the restaurant job, I can work at the bakery. I love to bake, and I could fill in anywhere they need help."

"See? Now you're thinking. And you would need to live over here, so you could move in with me. Done."

"Stop. I was just thinking out loud. I'll agree to go home, make peace with my dad, show you the beach, and then I'm coming back to make up with Bev. Then I can find my mom."

"Whatever you say," I said. But my mind was working overtime, thinking of how to get her in my bed every night.

I guess I was staying in this cesspool of a city for a while longer . . . but I wasn't losing my shitkickers.

"Come on. Let's take Tuck out, and then I have some plans for you." With her hand in mine, I helped Emerson up from the couch.

"You do?" she asked, one eyebrow waggling.

"How do you do that?"

"I don't know. My dad does it. I guess it's hereditary."

"I can't wait to meet this guy."

Emerson snorted out a laugh. "I'm sure he doesn't feel the same about you."

CHAPTER
TWENTY-FOUR

Emerson

Well, I was completely wrong. My dad seemed to adore everything about Price. Who knew?

We drove down on Friday. After giving Tuck a short walk, we hit the road before dawn. Price wanted as much time in the sand as possible.

As for me, I could have stalled. The inevitable fight with my dad loomed over me like a dark sky on a beach day. Of course, there hadn't been a need for me to pack a bag. All my beach stuff was still at home—where I'd abandoned it.

Along with my dad.

My dad sounded excited—or at least he faked it—when I called from the car to say I was visiting for the weekend and bringing a friend. Now that we were here, I saw he was genuinely over the freaking moon. When I told him I was bringing a guy and my dad didn't even balk, I should have known there was something up. What the heck? Didn't he remember Robby?

"Tell me more about your farm," Dad said to Price over a cold beer.

They were sitting on the porch, their feet kicked up on the railing, cold ones in hand. As for me, I was an afterthought on the porch swing, sipping on a lemon water with Tuck at my side. I just pumped my feet every now and again, letting the ocean breeze invade my pores, and watched my dad fall for Price like I had.

A small niggle of worry hit me. What would happen when Price went back to his beloved farm?

"It's pretty small as farms go, but we have a fruitful apple orchard and a good many dairy cows. We also raise pumpkins, and Mom makes pies and jellies."

Dad nodded, looking impressed. "I'm sure it's bigger than you think. Sounds like quite the operation."

"Eh, I guess. I do love it. Thought I'd be there forever, but I'm adjusting to New York. Hated it in the beginning, but it's changing for me. Certainly, I never thought I'd be getting a fancy degree. Not sure what I'll do with it, though. I exactly can't see myself on Wall Street."

My dad raised an eyebrow. "Yeah, the ties could be strangling after a while, huh? And I suspect your liking New York more has something to do with my daughter?"

"Ha!" Price let out a loud laugh before taking another swig of beer.

It was a regular Boys' Night Out before my very eyes.

"Definitely on the ties," he said, still chuckling. "Not my thing. I'm thinking about something bigger. Something with an impact on this world. Combining shit—I mean *crap*—I learned on the farm, and whatever they teach me in school. As for the city, yep, it's growing on me, thanks to your daughter. I'm sure you have your concerns, but I'll tell you this. I'm a good guy. I know I'm a bit older than her, but I'm telling you the truth—I'm into her. I really like her for all that is Emerson . . . sir."

"Sir? Cut the crap. Call me Bend," my dad said as he side-eyed my . . . boyfriend? Friend with benefits? Lover?

"Okay, no prob," Price said.

"So, you got a thing for my girl?" My dad lifted his beer to his lips and polished it off in one swig.

"How 'bout that humidity here in Jersey?" I blurted, unable to stop myself. I didn't know how we got to this point in the conversation, but I wanted it to stop. Needed it to.

"Quit it, Emerson. You brought this guy home, and I appreciate he's sharing his intentions."

"Oh my God! Dad!" I stood up, the swing flying back behind me. Tuck jumped down beside me, scared to death.

"Jesus, Em. You're freaking the damn dog out," my dad said as Price sat there watching, smirking, silently laughing.

"Dad!" I glared at him. "Do you remember why I left?"

"Yeah, because of that no-good, piece-of-you-know-what, Robby."

"Um . . ." I tugged at my messy bun and pulled it out.

Another smirk crossed Price's face—he knew he had the advantage. *Jerk.*

"Dad, you were the one all buddy-buddy with him when I left. Or did you forget?" I paced back and forth, the small porch not giving me a lot of room to cover.

My father's lips twitched. "Yeah, better to keep the enemy closer. You weren't talking to me, and I had to make sure you weren't running into that little shit's arms. He's a piece of work, running up there to see you. Next thing I know, the idiot's crying in his coffee over you and some guy. I had to bite the inside of my cheek to keep myself from laughing."

I turned away from him, my fists clenched. The desire to grunt and stomp my feet was almost impossible to resist.

"Christ. Was I played?" I said without turning around.

"Language," my dad said, gently chastising me.

"You were, babe." Price came up behind me, whispering in my ear, his arm around my waist. Then he turned to look at my dad. "There's no father in America who would like that guy for his daughter, right?"

"You're my kind of person," Dad told Price. "Let's have another beer."

And . . . boom, everything was dropped.

That's pretty much how Friday evening went. My dad being his straightforward, easygoing self, bonding with Price.

We ordered in pizza, which we ate on the porch, and after my dad went inside, Price asked me to take a walk on the beach. We'd seen it during daylight, dipping our toes on arrival, Price mesmerized by the crowds and the waves. He'd flopped himself down on a beach blanket earlier and declared, "I'm going to have you on this sand."

My fingers, spine, and the rest of my body tingled at the prospect of that being now.

Earlier, we had to leave Tuck at the house. Now, we leashed him up, stuck our feet in flip-flops, and headed for the short walk to the sand.

"I love it here," Price said while holding my hand. "Honestly, I didn't know what to expect. Of course, growing up, I wanted to see the ocean, but it wasn't a huge deal. Now I know what I was missing. Wonder if I would feel the same about Orlando? I've never been to see the big mouse either."

"It's not as exciting when you grow up here. Town empties out at the end of the season. You learn not to make friends with the seasonal kids. They leave . . . like my mom. I guess my dad made that mistake, and lived to regret it."

Price squeezed my hand. "Not when he got you. Aren't you glad you came home? See how it wasn't a big deal? He's your father . . . he's not allowed to stay mad at you forever."

"How did you get so wise, Mr. Barnes?" I half joked.

"Look, I may not be into this whole scenario with my dad, but I grew up respecting my mom more than anything. My stepdad made sure of that. He'd kick my ass if I back-talked her or didn't take her advice. She always told me, *I'm your mom . . . it's my job to do right by you, but I love you no matter what. Even when we have words.*"

"Aw." My eyes teared up. "That's the sweetest. I grew up wanting a mom like yours. I guess I got a dad instead."

We reached the beach entrance and kicked off our flip-flops, then hiked up and over the dunes, and I sort of hoped we were dropping the heavy conversation.

"You have a lot to be thankful for, Em," Price said, squeezing my hand again. "Your dad loves you. Take pride in that."

"I am, I guess. Truthfully, I thought it would be more dramatic, but you saw . . . my dad acted like nothing when we arrived. And now you guys are BFFs. Throwing Robby out the window."

Price stopped and turned me toward him. "Pretty fucking sure that Robby did that to himself. And right or wrong, your dad kind of played you with that. Knew what he was doing. Made sure you didn't end up in the wrong hands. I'd die for a dad like that. Look at us—you have the dad I always dreamed about, and I have the mom you wanted. I guess, together, we make the perfect pair."

A lump of regret formed in my throat, making my eyes burn. "I shouldn't have ignored my dad all summer. He's pretty good. The best."

"Hey." Price lifted my chin. "He knows you're growing up, and now you found me. So, yeah."

His lips met mine before he finished his own sentence. We stayed like that for a long while, beer on his breath, the moon in the background, Tuck digging in the sand by our feet.

"Thanks for bringing me. I didn't know it, but I needed something to cheer me up after the shitty time I had in Philly. I never should've gone there to see my dad. Should've gone to see my mom."

I eased my lips along his neck, standing on my tiptoes. "Hey, you didn't know. You're trying. That's all you can do."

"He's a no-good prick. I don't want anything to do with him, or anything or anyone related to him. I've gotta get out of that damn apartment."

"Come on, let's walk a bit," I told him as Tuck chased his tail by our feet. "Look, you have a free place to live, and you're getting your degree. Your mom wants that for you, so think of it that way."

He nodded. "Let's talk about you. You're done at the Bangladeshi place . . . thank fuck . . . and now you're going to ask Bev for a job. But what's the end game?"

"I don't know. I was thinking some sort of trade. Culinary. That way I could work anywhere. I don't know how much longer I can afford New York."

"So, you'll move in with me, make that ostentatious place feel more livable. Problem solved. My mom will be happy, so you can't say no."

"Quit it."

"I'll talk to your dad about it tomorrow. I know he's worried about your safety . . . that should seal the deal."

"Grrr, Price, don't you dare."

"Now it's on!"

I didn't have time to argue because he swiftly lifted me, laid me down in the sand, and kissed the heck out of me. The gritty shit dug into every crease and crevice—but I didn't care.

"Think your dad's asleep?"

"You're not sneaking into my room!"

"We'll see."

I wondered how my dad would like hearing that. With the way things had gone down, he probably wouldn't care.

CHAPTER
TWENTY-FIVE

Price

"Have a minute?" Emerson's dad found me in the kitchen the next morning, helping myself to some coffee.

"Hope this is okay?" I held up my mug.

"Yeah, that's what it's there for . . . to drink."

I nodded and took a swig before saying, "Thanks."

"So, I've been nice, and I like you, kid. But don't go thinking you can take advantage of my daughter," he said, eyeing me over the rim of his own mug.

Of course Bend wanted to make himself and his expectations known . . . but I liked this dude. He didn't pull his cock out to do it.

"Yes, sir, I get where you're coming from, and I appreciate you telling me like a grown-ass man. I don't think my own father would've been as diplomatic."

"Well, good for me . . . and my daughter. You're an all-right guy."

"Ha. You mean the apple *does* fall far from the tree."

He topped off his mug and looked at me. "I don't know your dad, but if I was him, I'd be damn proud of you."

Leaning my ass into the counter, I shrugged. "I don't know him all that well either. He was never really around, Mr. Bender."

Staring me down, he said, "Call me Bend, will ya? Look, some situations can't be avoided. We don't know why some parents do what they do, but they do it. Doesn't make it right. Look at Emerson's mom. I never thought I'd meet a woman who didn't want her own baby, but then it happened."

We were just two dudes, shooting the breeze, talking serious, and drinking coffee.

I wondered if it would have been like this with my dad if he'd been around. Bruce was cool and a great stepdad, but he always trod carefully with me, afraid to overstep.

"Yeah, I guess you're right. My mom's been a saint. Raised me to be a gentleman. All I ever shared with my good ole dad was my last name and some Middle Eastern bloodlines, hence the olive skin. Price freaking Barnes."

For a moment, Bend rubbed his chin and closed his eyes, looking pained, but then he snapped out of it. "He was from New York? Your dad?"

"Not originally, but he settled there. His mom was where his Middle Eastern roots came from. His dad was Irish, so his last name kept him in good graces, I always assumed."

"Got it." Bend picked up his mug, glancing at me. "So, what do you and my daughter have planned for today?"

I didn't get a chance to answer because the aforementioned daughter popped into the kitchen, clad in only a bikini, a stark contrast to my plaid pajama bottoms.

"Wave jumping, picnic lunch, letting Tuck roll in the sand," she said, bopping through the kitchen toward the coffeemaker.

"How about some shorts and a T-shirt?" her dad asked.

"Dad, I live at the beach. This is pretty much how I run around half the year. If you mean because of Price, you should see how some of the girls dress at the bar. This is fully clothed," she said with a giggle.

"I'll bet," Bend said, but he seemed to have an extra eye on me and how I responded.

"Why don't you grab some shorts and a tank," I said. "And flip-flops. I'll be ready to go in a few."

Hey, I wasn't a father, and I barely had one myself, so how was I to know what this all felt like in someone's gut?

"By the way, you don't need your boots!" Emerson tossed back at me.

"Uh, yeah, I know. Maybe you'll get a pair? We can be twins."

"We'll see. I prefer my flippies." Giving me a quick wink, she skipped out of the room. Not sure I'd ever seen this lighthearted version of Emerson, but I definitely dug it.

"Hurry up. I'm waiting," I called after her. When she was gone, I turned to Bend. "I was kidding. I'd wait all day for her. In case you were worried."

"I wasn't, kid," Bend said, seeming to vibe with me, and I can't say I wasn't happy. "I never believed in kismet, but maybe now I do . . ."

He didn't finish his thought as he guzzled his coffee and sauntered out of the room.

I couldn't help but wonder if he was only referring to my asking Emerson to put on clothes, or if it was something else. Mostly, I was relieved that he seemed to like me, and considered the visit a job well done on my part.

CHAPTER
TWENTY-SIX

Emerson

The rest of the weekend was pretty much the same, with the bromance in full swing between my dad and Price. He was even referring to my dad as Bend. No joke.

When they weren't hanging, Price was trying to seduce me every second. Now, *that* I liked. It might be a bit new to me, but I knew one thing—what I'd had with that sleaze, Robby, was nothing compared to this.

"Come on." Price grabbed my hand. He had a blanket under one arm, a bag of fries in his other hand, and Tuck at his feet. "Okay, buddy, you're staying here."

Price released my hand for a second to pat Tuck's head, and the damn dog seemed to act like he knew what Price really wanted. *Me.*

My dad and Price had walked to a small strip of shops earlier, grabbing a six-pack, and apparently the famous beach french fries. After catching them having a heart-to-heart about Lord knows what this morning, I'd almost offered to join them. But they'd given me that look, the *this is a guy thing* look. So I'd stayed behind. There was no way I could deal with whatever else they might have discussed.

While my dad was in the kitchen, fixing the sink with a beer next to him, Price and I had a rendezvous on the dunes for our last night. Settled on the blanket on the sand, hidden from view, Price reached over and fed me a fry.

"Um, these are good," I murmured, teasing him, keeping my distance, our thighs barely touching.

He plopped one in his own mouth. "They are."

"Mmm." I snatched another one.

"You know what's better?"

"Hmm?"

"You," he said.

Price leaned over and kissed me, and the next think I knew, he was spread over me. No sand in my back this time, thanks to his planning.

"I wonder what my dad thought when you grabbed the blanket," I joked, running my hand through the back of his hair.

"Babe, I think you're forgetting he had a shit fit when he heard about your apartment, and more than agreed you should live with me."

Suspicions confirmed. They'd been discussing me on their walk—and probably earlier.

With Price's lips so close to mine as he spoke, I'm not going to lie—mine burned as I waited for him to kiss me again, and my concentration was ruined.

"Well, you certainly set me up for that. I just can't get over my dad. I thought all these rules were about me. I guess he saw right through Robby."

Price ground into me. "Let's not talk about that dipshit when I'm on top of you."

His mouth met mine again, his tongue slipping inside, lightly touching mine. I loved his easy exploration of me, his patience with my inexperience, and the way he helped me find my own way.

I couldn't describe it. I just felt it.

His hand slipped under my shirt and over my bra, his thumb caressing the satin covering my nipple. I moaned . . . maybe too loud.

"Shhh," Price told me. "When we get home, and I send Johnny to get your shit, you can moan as loud as you want. But here, we don't want to get caught."

"Johnny?"

"Yep, I'm becoming a true New Yorker, having people do my shit. Look what you're doing to me." He nibbled on my lip and pushed his hardness against me.

"Don't blame this on me," I said, and my words came out panting, wanton.

"Nah, I'm kidding. I have class on Monday, and I can't miss it. Plus, I don't want you going back there ever. So, Johnny likes to do what he gets paid for."

"Stop, you're making me crazy. I can do it," I said, squeezing his butt.

"I'll stop when you're settled. In my place. Or maybe when I find my own goddamn place."

"This is nuts. I've known you two seconds, and now I'm moving in with you. I can't do that."

I felt myself sink a little deeper into the sand, like my feelings sank a little deeper for Price. He was like quicksand, though. I was sinking deeper and deeper, falling for him hard.

"Yep, you're moving in. I'll dress up like the bunny in your bar, if that makes you feel better . . . more at home."

His kisses were soft, closed mouthed, promising. I wanted more, harder.

"I'm not quitting the bar, I'll have you know."

"It's fine, Johnny can take you. And you can pack. Happy?"

"Ugh, you'd better kiss me again. I don't like where this convo is going."

He obliged and more. Slipping his hand inside my shorts, he made sure his thumb found the right spot. I went off, not sure how he did that, especially so quickly. Not one to argue, I savored his fingers on me, inside me, our mouths fused.

"You sure about the condom thing? I'm clean," he said, drawing me out of my haze. "I don't want to ever push you to do something before you're ready."

"Except move in."

This sassiness got me thoroughly kissed. Tongue-twisting, hungry, *can't get enough of me and my snark* kissed.

"Yes, I'm sure," I said when we broke apart. "When my dad didn't know what to do with my periods, he had a neighbor take me to the doctor. They gave me the pill to regulate me. I'm clean too." I winked, not able to help myself.

Price left my shirt on but lifted it to kiss my chest. He ran his hot breath over my bra, until he came to my belly button, where his tongue swirled. His hand quickly took care of removing my shorts and panties, and he shrugged off his own shorts.

"Commando?" I asked.

"You bet."

And then he was inside me, and I forgot all about the fact that I was going to live with him at the encouragement of my dad, and Johnny was going to take me to get my stuff. For a few minutes, Bev hopefully waiting for me to make up with her didn't cross my mind. Of course, I still wanted to find my mom, but she was way back in the recesses of my brain.

At this moment, all I wanted to do was feel Price, to be with him in every way.

CHAPTER
TWENTY-SEVEN

Emerson

Monday night, I walked into the Lucky Artist Bakery, sweaty and worn out from moving, but the task at hand was too important to skip. I'd forgotten the significance of Monday until I shuffled through the door and mumbled *shit* to myself.

I'm important to Bev.

"Hey," I said to my friend, whose back was to me as she fiddled with the cappuccino maker.

She turned and said, "Hi."

Huh. So that's all she's going to give me. She's going to make me work for it.

I reminded myself not to drop the glass jar in my hand and make a mess. "Here," I said, sliding it toward her over the counter. The shells inside tinkled and rattled.

"What's this?"

As she eyed me, I smoothed my hair back into my messy bun. "I made it at the shore this weekend. It's just some shells I collected. A peace offering, I guess. A stupid one, but I didn't know what to do."

"It's pretty." She picked it up and placed it under the painting that started this shit. Paula's whimsical coffee cup was anything but frivolous.

"Look, Bev, I'm really sorry. I didn't come looking for you. When I came in here the first time, I thought of it as a lucky break. Some kind of luck, or the gods looking out for me. Now I've come to think of it as a sick coincidence. Shit luck."

She didn't interrupt or disagree, so I kept talking.

"What I didn't count on was meeting you, finding the first true friend I've made in a long time. You became a good friend quickly, and I think that's because we have a great connection. But I shouldn't have lied . . . by omission or otherwise. I should have told you what I was thinking from the minute I saw that painting," I said, glancing at it and then back to her.

We still stood opposite each other, the metal counter nothing compared to the emotional divide between us.

"Let's sit down." Bev untied her apron and started to pour two coffees, but then paused. "You want it iced? You look like you've had a day."

Her small, caring comment surrounded my body in warmth, like I was wrapped in a bulky blanket in winter.

"No, hot is good."

Bev walked around, and I took in the flour dusting her leggings and her greasy ponytail as we sat at a small table.

"Why aren't you at dance?" I decided to bring it up, knowing it was a sacrifice for her to be here.

"Couldn't go today. Fred, the guy who was doing the baking, got a full-time gig over at Eataly he couldn't say no to. So I'm covering baking my mom's recipes and the counter. We have an ad up for a counter person and a part-time baker. My mom wants to come back, but I still think she needs to get her strength and cleared."

"I hate that you had to miss dance."

As she shrugged and leaned against the counter, I thought she looked tired. This was too much for a young woman like Bev. She should be falling in love, going to bars, dancing, having fun.

"Well, I have other news. I moved in with Price."

"What?" Her head popped up, and she shrieked.

"It's a long story, but here's the abbreviated version. He convinced me to go home, make up with my dad, and of course, he wanted to go with me. So we did, and, yeah, my dad fell for him."

I couldn't help rolling my eyes while I said it.

"Then he told my dad about how the Bangladeshi restaurant replaced me with a relative, and he convinced my dad my living arrangements weren't up to snuff. Price pretty much roped me into moving in with him." I gulped my coffee like it was water. "So, I need this caffeine more than anything, because today I moved in while Price went to see some professors. Oh crap," I said suddenly, remembering Johnny idling outside.

I held up a finger.

"One sec," I said to Bev, then shot up and ran to the door. I waved at Johnny, and he got out of the car. "I'll take an Uber," I called out, and he nodded and waved back.

"Living the good life, I see," Bev said when I made it back to the table.

"Oh, shush." I knew she was joking. "Anyway, what I'm getting at is, I told Price I was hoping to take some culinary classes. And if you wanted, maybe I could help you at the bakery? If you accept my apology and want to stay friends? I'd do baking or handle the counter or both. I'm still bartending, but I need the money. Price has a lot of these . . . trappings," I said, not knowing what else to call his lifestyle. "But they're not mine."

"Really?" Bev smiled for the first time since I came in.

"Yeah, really."

"That would be awesome. I know my mom would be so glad to have you."

Addressing the elephant that sat on the table between us, I said, "What about you?"

"Come on, it's over. Give me a hug. I've missed you." Standing, she pulled me for a huge hug.

Wrapped in her arms, I said, "Under one condition. You don't skip dance on Mondays anymore."

"With you here, I won't." She gave me another squeeze before releasing me. "Now, tell me all the good stuff. About your dad, and Price . . ."

"I will. But I want to—have to—say one more thing." I wrung my hands like a groom with jitters. "I'm still going to look for my mom. I have to. Otherwise, it will bother me forever. Your mom said she may be able to get me an address."

Bev nodded. "Of course I don't want to take that away from you. I also don't want you to hurt any more than you already do. I've learned to live without my dad, and it's for the best. But I get that we're two different people."

"I admire you," I said, and my gaze dropped to the shiny floor. "I wish, really, honestly, I do . . . I wish I could be like you, and say I'm better off and move on. But I can't. This has become too big for me. I have to find out what happened with my mom."

Bev ran her hand down my arm and wrapped my fingers in hers. "I get it."

CHAPTER
TWENTY-EIGHT

Price

"Morning." My lips ran along the nape of Emerson's neck while my hand lifted her hair, the long strands sifting through my fingers. It was the most delicious moment, topping sitting on the edge of the water tower watching the sunset, cold beer in hand, a soft thigh next to mine.

I'd finally found my happy place in this godforsaken city. In the arms—and limbs—of a woman, a very young woman. Not the happy place I'd expected, but I wanted it and took it anyway.

Emerson grumbled into her pillow. I knew she was awake because she'd been pushing her ass back into me for ten minutes.

"I like having you here."

"You've said," she said, turning in my arms.

"Can't help it. For some reason, when it comes to you, all my moves go out the fucking window. I'm helplessly smitten . . ." My lips lightly brushed hers. "With these," I mumbled against her mouth.

"Morning breath," she warned.

"Don't care."

Her hair a tangled mess, both her tiny-ass camisole and sleep shorts riding up and twisted, she looked like she belonged here in this fortress apartment. I wished she'd stay forever . . .

What am I thinking?

"And these," I said, my hand ghosting under her sleep shorts, lingering over her heat.

"Mmm." She pushed into me, and I gave her a little more pressure.

My tongue found her neck and ran a path to her ear. I stopped there and sucked on her earlobe, my hand doing its top-of-the-clothing work below. Ignoring her earlier warning about bad breath—she was so full of shit, nothing was bad about Emerson—I found her mouth again. As I sucked on her lip, she opened for my tongue, and it was on.

It didn't take long for her to go off in my arms. Her core grinding into my palm, her mouth making love to mine, her chest expanding and falling with quick breaths. It was a glorious sight, and I wanted to wake up to it every day.

"This is so crazy. I can't believe I live here, that I just woke up to that, that this is my reality. My daily," she said, falling back into her pillow.

"You've been here for days. You should be used to it by now, don't you think?"

"Are you counting? Looking for a way to get me out?" Her hand slid down my chest, tickling along the way, her smooth palm finding my hardness.

"Never," I said on a groan.

Her hand didn't still. She grazed me gently, teasing. I waited for her to pick up speed on her own.

"I still want to look for a different place. After classes really get under way, I'm going to chat with my dad about moving to my own apartment, one that's more me. Maybe with an outdoor spot for Tuck. Taking him out in the morning is a pain in the ass. On the farm, we'd just open the door and let them out while the coffee was brewing. But there's some cool spots here . . . warehouses. I've seen them on my runs."

"Mr. New York."

She teased me, her hand on my dick, but I didn't mind. Although her words socked me in the gut.

"Nah, farm boy at heart. But both women in my life think I should get my degree, so I'm embracing that."

"Is that so? Both women?" She squeezed me tighter, her hand working me faster.

"You and my mom, but I'm not in the mood to talk about her now."

I lifted Emerson's top leg over my hip, creating a delicious friction between us. I moved her hand out of the way and teased myself with her heat.

"Mmm, uh-huh." She moaned into my ear, leaning in, kissing along my neck, leaving goose bumps in her wake. "Though, I know you're distracting me. It may be my first time living with a guy, sleeping with a guy . . . crap, doing everything for the first time with a guy, but I'm smart. Despite the fact I'm rambling. I know what you're doing."

Her soft lips still grazed my skin, sending a chill down my spine.

My heart pounded furiously at her words. Emerson was giving me all her major firsts, and here I was saying that the city wasn't enough for me. I wanted to go back to my farm, live the life I'd set out to live, maybe not be the best version of myself.

At that thought, my body stilled.

"Hey, what's going on inside that head?" She tapped my forehead with her finger and stared at me.

"Sorry. I got distracted thinking about where I could move," I lied, sort of. But I had to tread carefully. Here I was wishing this woman would be in my bed forever, and yet I was still homesick.

I had to find a way to merge my two worlds—my love of the farm, and this woman in this gargantuan city. Of course, it occurred to me that the person with a solution would be my mom. I made a mental note to go home for a day or two and discuss it with her.

Until then, though, I wanted to get inside Emerson.

Enough of this talking.

My hand found its way back down toward her core, making sure she was still more than ready. Panting in my ear, sweat dampening the back of her neck when I ran my other hand under her mane, she whispered my name in a silent plea. I didn't wait, finding myself deep inside her, taking my time, making delicious morning love to Emerson.

Yep, I'd have to do whatever it took to merge both of my loves. Farm life and Emerson Bender.

"Gin fizz," I shouted from the end of the bar, my elbows leaning on the hardwood.

"Cool it, buddy," some douche said next to me.

I didn't even look his way. Just brushed my hair out of my eyes and focused on my girl.

Instead of the cocktail I requested, Emerson set a beer in front of me. I winked and tossed a twenty on the bar, which she promptly shoved back at me.

"Hey, that's not even what he ordered. Can I get some service?" the douche demanded.

"When the woman behind the bar is yours, you get your drink first." I tipped my beer bottle toward him and moved to the back of the bar to catch a preseason football game on TV.

"Okay, caveman," he shouted back at me.

His words didn't bother me, although I'm sure Emerson was shooting daggers at me. I didn't look back at him, not caring. No way was I going to let some pompous shit talk that way to me or her.

Despite it being Thursday, the bunny was running—or hopping—around, making a fool of himself. Going up to girls and dancing with them, shaking his tail. I rolled my eyes and went back to the game.

I didn't like Emerson still coming over here to work, but if there was anything I'd learned from my mom, it's that you can't steamroll a woman. And I'd already talked Emerson into enough. So, I was here keeping an eye on her, bossing douches around.

If I had my way, next up for Em would be culinary school. She was loving being at the bakery this week. Imagine if she could do it long-term? I'd have to talk with her dad. He'd be game for it.

Her dad loved me after a few days. He got that I had her best interests at heart.

Damn straight. But what about mine?

Shit, I didn't want to dwell on it. Luckily, my phone beeped, taking me away from my deep thoughts. Or not.

It was Bruce in a group text with Moira and me.

I rubbed my forehead and mumbled an obscenity or two. I hadn't bothered to fill in either him or my mom on the status change with Moira, or the fact that I'd moved a chick into my grand digs. *Okay, not a chick, but you know what I mean.*

Hoping you can come home this weekend for our anniversary. I'm going to make a small dinner at the house. My ribs, which you know are damn edible.

My mom must be missing me. A wave of guilt washed over me, and I took a big gulp of my beer, reminding myself that she wanted me here.

Of course Bruce would include Moira. We hadn't had a family occasion without her in years. But that was before my dad rode in on his white horse, wielding his sword—I mean, *deep pockets*—and demanded I move to New York.

I'll be there.

That's all I responded. I'd call Bruce tomorrow and explain my new living situation. Heck, my new feelings. I wanted to bring another girl home, and they needed to know about it.

Not sure how I would handle the Moira situation, but our relationship had run its course. Nobody successfully marries their high school sweetheart and lives to tell happy stories about it. Right?

Goddamn, I was even becoming cynical like a New Yorker.

"What's up?"

I felt arms slide around me, and I turned and placed a kiss on Em's lips. "Hey, you catch a break over there? They let you out from behind the bar?"

"Yeah, it's slammed tonight. Bunny's even here. Everyone is back from their beach trips, and school's started."

She leaned into me, and my phone buzzed again.

Of course, Moira.

I'll be there! Happy anniversary, Bruce. See you this weekend, P! Yay! Oh, I'll bring peanut butter pie.

"Something I'm missing?" Emerson might be younger, but she didn't miss much. Her eyebrow cocked, she looked me dead in the eye.

"My parents' anniversary . . . Mom's with Bruce, I mean. There's a dinner this weekend. Want to come with?" I tried to go for casual and not guilty. Although I wasn't guilty, but I knew how it looked. How it felt.

"What about the girl bringing the peanut butter pie, P?"

My initial popping off Emerson's tongue was the worst sound ever. I liked when she moaned my name, her head fallen back, breathing heavy for me and only me.

"The ex. I guess no one clued my parents in on us severing things."

"Not even you? And what about me? They don't know about me?" Hurt radiated off her, but Emerson was too proud to admit it. Instead, she turned this fight into a coy joke.

I pulled her in between my legs, uncrossed her arms from in front of her chest, and placed her hands on my shoulders. Looking her straight in the eye, I said, "I'm more of an actions-first, talk-later kind of guy. But don't mistake this tiny communication snafu for a lack of feelings from me. I'm crazy for you, Emmy B. And no one—not my ex, not my mom, or my fucking bio dad who I barely know, or your dad who I happen to love, or your asshat ex, or even a goddamn peanut butter pie—is going to keep me from falling for you."

She stared at me, processing my direct words.

"Anything you want to say?" I joked back with her, even though the pounding in my chest was anything but funny.

Emerson looked down and put her hand in mine. I loved this about her. The need to touch, the desire to move on. She wasn't a psycho girl who held on to grudges.

"I have to work this weekend. Randy is off, and I promised. Especially since we went to the beach last weekend. Plus, I'm also running the bakery on Sunday, and I was kind of hoping, praying I'd find out my mom's address. Sheila's been promising it."

"Well . . ."

"Before you get all Mr. Fix-It . . . no, you can't make up the money I wouldn't make working and bulldoze my plans. I want to meet your mom, but I have to take a rain check. Plus, I'm more of an apple girl when it comes to pie. So, I'll come next time, when there's no potential peanut butter pie or the girl who's making it. 'Kay?"

Emerson was going to shrug it off, despite her obviously bruised feelings. What was that about? There was so much I still needed to figure out about this woman. *This woman who lives with me.*

I stood and placed my lips on her forehead. "Was that our first fight?" I made a game-time decision to run with her plan to make light of this.

"I don't know." She slapped my arm and then pinched my bicep. "I'd hardly call it a fight. More like me being cool and you being a jerk."

"Ha. Whatever you say."

"Do we get to make up?" She leaned in and placed a quick kiss on my jaw. "I have to get back to the bar, but later . . ."

"Oh, I like the sound of later."

CHAPTER
TWENTY-NINE

Emerson

Friday night, I tiptoed into the apartment after two o'clock in the morning.

"No one's here," I whispered to myself. "Wait, why am I whispering?"

I'd lived with Price all week, and was already in the habit of being quiet when I came in. Maybe because he insisted on Johnny driving me to and from the bar.

"For God's sake, the guy makes more money than I do. He shouldn't be driving me," I said, talking to myself again.

I slipped off my shoes by the fridge and poured a glass of water before making my way to pee and take a shower. I was exhausted, but still wished Price had left Tuck. I could have used the company and the walking buddy.

As I turned on the water in the bathroom, my phone buzzed on the counter.

Home?

You know I am.

I was sure he had Johnny text after he dropped me off. And, yes, part of me was still mad over the ex-girlfriend thing, even though I didn't show it. I mean, why was she still going to the anniversary dinner? And baking a pie? A peanut butter pie? The questions were endless.

Yeah, but I wanted you to tell me.

Of course, he added a winky emoji. Eh, I was still sort of pissed.

Exhausted. Water running for shower.

I heard the phone buzz again, but I was already naked and standing under the water. He'd have to wait.

As the showerhead literally rained down on me, I turned over dessert creations in my head. Recipes that involved apples . . . maybe Price could help me with the selection? I wouldn't make anything with peanut butter.

God, I'm messed up.

Soaping my hair, I closed my eyes and let my mind wander to things other than dessert. Price touching me, sliding down onto his knees, his tongue skimming me, making me want more. It would build slowly, reaching a crescendo . . . until I came apart.

Reminding myself that I was the one living with Price in this ridiculous apartment—not her, the ex—I jumped out of the shower and read Price's text.

Too bad I'm not there. Miss you.

Miss you too. And Tuck. And your pancakes.

I added a few emojis—a heart, a stack of pancakes, and an eggplant.

To which he sent me a blueberry, a dog, and a peach.

Mission accomplished. I laughed out loud.

Night, night.

I typed out the text quickly, tugged on a T-shirt of Price's, and crawled into the gigantic California king by my lonesome. Snuggling with both of my bedmate's pillows, I was out in minutes.

As I was working the counter at the bakery on Sunday, Bev rushed in, tears streaming down her face, her bright orange raincoat lopsided, the buttons off kilter, her hair sopping from the rain.

"We have to close up now," she said, her voice shaking. "It'll be fine. We'll donate the leftover product down the street. This is it, the end. Maybe a day or two."

"I can stay here," I told her. "I don't mind. Keep the place open regular hours and then close up. We'll stop baking, and I can sell off what's left. I'm happy to do that."

"You don't understand. My mom has something to tell you. She said, *'Bring Em back. I have the info she wants on Paula, her mom. And I need to tell her this.'* You don't get it . . . her time's running out, and I have to honor her every last request. Come on, Em. We have to go see my mom. Don't you want to know? That's what you came here for . . . to find your mom. Maybe we can find her, finally, and I can have a connection to my mom when she's gone. Maybe you can get her help."

During our tiff, Bev and I had missed each other. When we made up, I'd gone back to work on the premise we wouldn't discuss Paula. And now her mom wanted to get all Chatty Cathy on me? She still hadn't given me Paula's address as planned.

I couldn't relate to Bev's undying devotion to her mother, but it didn't mean I wasn't envious. A few months ago, last year, I would have given anything to meet my mom.

But now? Now I wasn't so sure I wanted to find her. I had Price and a good life, and I was starting to talk with my dad again. Maybe everyone was right—maybe this search wasn't worth it.

Practically turning green over Bev's relationship with her mom wasn't a good look for me, so I swallowed all my mixed emotions. "Of course I'd never stand in the way. If Sheila asked, let's go."

I untied my apron, set it on the counter, and flipped the sign to CLOSED before heading out the door with Bev. She'd stopped sobbing, but every breath was labored. She seemed to be dying alongside her mother, something else I'd never truly get, especially since Paula remained a mystery. I knew she existed. I knew she'd been married to a wealthy businessman and had fought a lifetime battle with addiction. She'd disappeared recently, but where to? No one had a fucking clue.

Perhaps that's what Sheila wanted to share with me.

"Come on," Bev said. "We'll take a cab. Like my mom keeps reminding me, I'm getting my inheritance early. The bakery will be all mine to do with what I want." She stood out in the street and threw her hand up in the air.

"Don't say things like that," I said, advising her from no personal experience whatsoever. I tried to channel Price. What would he say or do?

My heart ached like nothing I'd ever felt before in my life. Price had been back home at his beloved farm for only a few days, and my heart ached for him. The idea that he was spending time with his high school sweetheart worried me. He'd hated New York, and at one point, couldn't wait to get back home.

I just didn't understand why home meant so much to him. Home was just a place, right?

Once Bev and I reached their apartment, I was surprised to see how much Sheila had faded in the past week. She was sitting at their kitchen table, her face pale and thin, dark circles under her eyes.

Sheila handed me a slip of paper. "There—that's her address, the last place she lived before she went wherever she's been. She could be dead, for all I know."

Her hand shook when she handed it over. My mouth dropped open at her insensitive words, so unlike her.

"Mom!" Bev shrieked.

"She's only being honest. I don't know much about addiction, but I'm pretty sure my mom hurt yours in more ways than one. I'm sure she didn't mean to," I said, defending a woman I'd never met. "It was the drugs. I guess that's why she left me."

Sheila sighed. "I'm sorry, so sorry, girls. Bev's right. That wasn't fair. The chemo is messing with my sense of humor. Anyway, that was where Paula was staying after she got divorced. I only went there once or twice. She lived a bit like a hermit then, kept to herself. Partly because her marriage failed . . . and partly, I suspect, because she was using a lot."

"It's okay," I said. "Sad, but the truth hurts. I could be too late. I may have missed my chance. To be honest, I'm not even sure what I can do. Or what to say . . . *hey, mom, here I am!*"

"Don't say that," Sheila said, scolding me. "This is on me; I'm being down. Maybe I didn't try hard enough as her friend. But that man, he was her new beginning and demise all wrapped up in one. His money and his past became her worst enemies. She loved his money, but then it enabled her to get the good stuff and ignore all of us peons. And his past haunted him too."

"What do you mean?" Bev asked, still in her dance outfit, her orange raincoat now discarded.

"Look at the paper," Sheila told me.

A good night's sleep was 100 percent why my hand shouldn't be shaking right now. I'd not only had one but two great nights' sleep since Price left, a weekend to myself, and plenty of time to think about how much I wanted this very moment.

Shoving an errant hair behind my ear, I took a deep breath. On this folded piece of yellow lined paper was my best clue. My only real clue to finding the one person I'd wanted to meet since I realized all my friends had a mom and I didn't. This was my strongest lead. Maybe, finally, I was going to find my mom. I wanted to hold it close to my heart and rip it up at the same time. The tips of my fingers tingled.

I set it on the counter next to me. Opening the fold, sliding my palm along the creases, I stared at the address written in cursive. More like gaped, my mouth open wide, tears suddenly stinging my eyes.

I whipped my head up to stare at Sheila. "Is this some sort of joke?"

She shook her head, and Bev looked confused.

"What?" Bev snatched the paper from me. "So? It's some ritzy place on Central Park South. Are you shocked? We told you she found someone who had more money than she was raised with—"

"This is Price's address," I shrieked. "Where he lives, the apartment his dad bought for him. This is where I *live* with him."

"It's not a coincidence." Sheila looked at the tile floor in their kitchen. "Or a joke. I'm sorry, Emerson."

My world reeling, I stared at the kitchen floor with tear-filled eyes. Blurry swirls of black tiles mixed in with white made me dizzy.

"Why?" I half screamed, half whispered. Was this even possible?

"This is why I didn't want to give it you," Sheila said softly. "Why I dragged my feet."

Bev stood in front of me and shook me. "What the freak is going on?"

I was standing there, mumbling gibberish, still looking at the floor, feeling crazed.

"When you said your boyfriend's name was Price," Sheila said, "I became curious because it's an uncommon first name. Called a few friends. I knew the man Paula married had a son whose name was Price. Paula is gone, and I don't know where, but her ex-husband moved his son into her apartment about a couple months ago. They'd been estranged, and it had been an effort to reconnect."

I remember hearing Bev saying, "You need to sit down," and then everything went black.

Bev's voice came to me from what seemed like far away. "Em, open your eyes. You're gonna be okay. Open them, come on."

A cold cloth was pressed to my forehead.

"That feels good," I whispered. "Can I stay like this forever?"

"Oh, thank God. You passed out."

Bev continued to ramble on about how worried she was, and I still didn't open my eyes. As long as they were closed, my reality still included being in love with Price—and him loving me back—and not falling for the son of my missing mom's ex-husband.

"Come on, sweetie. Open your eyes," Bev told me.

I shook my head, stubbornly squeezing my eyes tight and pressing my lips together.

"This isn't going to change anything," she said gently. "With Price."

"It will," I mumbled. Opening my eyes, I looked at my friend. "You don't know. He had it out with his dad recently, and a few weeks before that. He's definitely been wanting to limit any and all contact with his dad. He hates him. Now I'm living with Price in this apartment, and he's going to think the same as you—that I orchestrated all of this to get close to my mom."

"This isn't your fault," she said as she sat me up, then helped me into a chair at the kitchen table.

"You thought it was, remember? And he told me to explain it to you, but I know he won't be as forgiving. He's a small-town guy at heart, who believes relationships are built on trust. He'll see me as a liar."

A sob jumped to my throat, begging to come out. "I lost my virginity in that apartment. I'm living there now, and all this time, it was my mom's. Why? Of all the guys, of all the damn apartments in this huge city, how did I fall for him and meet you? Christ, it's like a cruel joke. Like my mom is the guy behind the drape in the *Wizard of Oz*, and she's playing puppeteer or whatever, making me end up in this tangled mess."

"Shhh, you're letting yourself get carried away." Bev placed her hand on my shoulder, stilling me.

"All I wanted was to know my mom. Now I almost lost the only friend I made. And I most certainly will lose the guy I fell in love with. Oh, and guess what? I still don't know where my fucking mom is!"

Drained of words, I dropped my forehead onto Bev's shoulder and rid myself of all my tears too. She patted my back, rocking me back and forth until my sobs slowed and my sniffles died down.

After a while, I accepted a handful of tissues from Sheila and wiped my face, then blew my nose. Sniffling one last time, I choked out, "I have to call my dad. I messed everything up."

Bev and Sheila stood up and said they'd wait in the living room until I was done.

Both from broken homes, Bev and I were kindred spirits. She got me. I'd thought the same about Price, but now the situation was way different, and we were screwed.

"Dad," I cried into the phone. This was becoming a bad habit. I'd left to be more independent, and all I did was call my daddy, crying.

"What's wrong, baby?"

Hearing his voice only made me cry harder. I was supposed to be strong and independent. I am woman, hear me roar, and all that. For Christ's sake, I was raised by a single man, shouldn't that make me tough?

"Dad . . ." I sobbed out his name, my voice hoarse, wrung out with emotion.

"Emerson, are you okay?" His worry seemed to radiate through the phone.

"Mom, she used to live in Price's apartment, but I didn't know. I didn't fall for him because of that, I swear—"

"You don't have to prove anything to me, honey. I know you didn't."

"But he's going to think so," I wailed.

"I don't think so, baby girl. He's a wise kid. Wise beyond his years. In fact, when I finally put it all together—"

"What do you mean?" My question came out more as a shriek.

"Well, I had a hunch. When I was chatting with Price, he mentioned his name and how he was part Middle Eastern. I may be from a small town, but I'm not dumb. I knew what your grandpap found out. I knew who your mom married, and at the time, all that stuck with me was he was filthy rich. I can admit, I was jealous or envious, whatever. He had something I didn't."

My father's words rattled in my head, confusing me.

"Wait! This isn't about you now. You knew this about Price and me. Sheila too. And no one thought to tell me?"

"We were all protecting you, I guess. We knew you'd find out on your own terms. That is, I don't know Sheila, but I'm guessing."

"Crap, I have to put an end to all this craziness." Anger had replaced my sadness, and I felt a stubborn destructive streak coursing through my veins.

"I gotta go," I told my dad as Bev made her way back into the kitchen. I shooed her out with my hand.

"Em, listen to me. None of this is Price's fault. Do you hear me? Don't take this out on him."

Not really sure what I knew or what I heard, I knew what I had to do. After disconnecting the call, I marched out to Sheila and Bev's living room. "I'll be back. You stay."

"Wait!" they called out in unison, but I didn't listen.

CHAPTER
THIRTY

Price

"I'm back!" Finally back from Pennsylvania, I dropped my bag on the floor, disappointed that the apartment looked empty.

Emerson hadn't answered any of my texts all day. Not a single one. I knew she was working at the bakery, but it was closed for the day by now. Fucking Moira and that group text stuck in my gut like sour milk.

My greeting met silence, but the security alarm wasn't on, so I wondered if Emerson fell asleep. That had to be it.

"Em?" I called, walking toward the bedroom. My pulse raced, worry and regret pounding in my chest.

I stopped when I noticed a yellow sticky note on the counter.

I can't do this right now. It's not about you, but my mom.
Love always, E

"What the fuck?" I roared, crumpling the note and slamming my other hand onto the metal island.

I stalked toward the bedroom and found Emerson curled up in a ball on the bed, her eyes open, staring blankly into space. "Is this some sort of cruel joke? Emerson? What the fuck is going on?"

When she jerked back in the pillows, I immediately apologized.

"I'm sorry, I didn't mean to sound so gruff. But I just walked in on this note. This freaking note saying you can't do this."

"I can't," she whispered, and then started to cry.

"Hey." I sat down next to her, my hand finding purchase on her hip. Her eyes were open, so I didn't think she was sleep talking, but she hadn't said anything more. "You okay?"

My hand ran up and down her arm, and I noticed she was in dirty, sticky work clothes and shoes. But she still said nothing.

"Is this about the weekend? About Moira? I told her not to come to dinner. She got mad, but she didn't come. Wants to be friends and all that, but it's not going to work."

Finally, Emerson moved, shaking her head.

"Em? Babe, what's wrong?" I turned her to face me.

Her eyes puffy and red, she started to bawl. She couldn't get out a word out through the hiccupping sobs.

"Shhh, you have to calm down and tell me what's wrong. You're scaring the shit out of me." I pushed the damp hair out of her face and pulled her into my chest, but she continued to cry. "Emerson? Tell me what the fuck is going on?"

I was losing my patience. My own body began to shake. First the note, and now this.

"I . . . I have to move out of here," she croaked out. "I was going to just leave . . . the note. But I couldn't. I lay down in bed and all I could smell was you, and I couldn't make myself get up. And my dad said—"

"What? Why? What does your dad have to do with any of this?"

A million possibilities ran through my head. Money, jobs, moving back with her dad, leaving New York for good, Moira. Emerson could be lying about not caring. Maybe this was about her asshole ex . . . he could have weaseled his way back in.

"Em, you're not making any sense."

She shook her head, refusing to look up at me. "I have to go tonight. Now. That's pretty clear."

"You're talking crazy. It isn't like you to be mean like this."

Finally, Emerson showed some emotion. She gaped up at me, looking like someone had slashed her with a knife.

"Tell me what happened. Christ, I feel like I'm going to stroke out." Kicking off my boots—I'd come straight from the farm—I lay down the bed and slid in next to her, and for a second or two, I felt okay. "You don't have to go anywhere. I know this is new, and a lot, and maybe it's too soon to live together. But sometimes it happens. This is right. I get that it's overwhelming."

"I have to go," she said as a tear ran down her cheek. "I want you to know this, though . . . I care for you. I'm not being mean on purpose, I swear."

I swiped away her tears. "Em? What is all this?"

"I care about you. Too much, way too much. And this, all of this, living here, you taking me under your wing, giving me your affection . . ." Her words came out in hiccups, disjointed and crazy-sounding. "It's been incredible, and I was going to run out and only leave the note, but you deserve better. My dad said this wasn't your fault."

What wasn't my fault? I didn't know what any of this was about.

"Where is this coming from?" I cupped her cheek and looked into her eyes. Forcing myself to calm down, I decided to proceed carefully. My frustration wasn't helping anything.

She cleared her throat and spoke, her words raspy with emotion. "I have to go, that's *it*."

She gave me a tender, closed-mouth kiss. It felt like good-bye for fucking good, and I hated it. No way was I going to accept it.

"Emerson? Tell me, what the fuck?"

I didn't want to move, but I pulled back from her mouth. Standing up, I paced and took in the room. Nothing of hers was on the counter anymore, and there was a duffel in the corner.

"What the hell?"

Emerson dragged herself off the bed and to her feet, looking like a drunk on a bender. She went toward her bag and bent down, ignoring me.

"No!" It was the first time I'd raised my voice in this cuckoo-for-Cocoa-Puffs situation. I thought of my mom; she'd used the expression a lot when I was a teenager. But this was crazier than anything I'd done back then.

A growl emanated from Emerson's chest, and I was glad to hear it. Finally, some damn emotion from her other than crying.

"I. Am. Going."

"I see that," I bit out, my tone curt.

"Don't look at me like I'm crazy. I'm doing this for you. I adore you. Adore, do you hear me? I'm trying to be strong. Mature."

"Mature? You're running away from me!" Sweat beaded my brow. I cracked my knuckles to keep myself from punching a hole in the wall. I had to remind myself I wasn't in a barn anymore—I was in a penthouse with the woman I was falling for, a very young woman who was acting her age.

Shit. I had to remember Emerson's inexperience in matters of the heart. Her tough outer shell could be so deceiving. But it didn't matter. I cared for enough for her to wade through this shit—whatever the fuck it was.

"You're doing this for me? Come again? Me?" I leaned back against the wall and watched her face fall. Damn straight, she wasn't the only one who could cause pain. Squeezing my eyes shut, I hated myself for it, though.

Emerson gave me a bleak look. "Yes, you. Why? Because your dad is . . . *was* . . . married to my mom. He loves her. He does. And she's nothing but a problematic bitch. Shocker, she doesn't love him back, like she did with me too. And now, spoiler alert, he's chasing her around like I am. Your dad and I are one and the same, desperate for the love of a woman who can't give it."

My mind raced as I stared at her. "What? Where the hell did you get that? Are you hallucinating? I don't even fucking know my dad. He roared into my life and then basically walked back out."

Emerson shook her head. "This isn't about you. It's about me. I hate to tell you all this. It makes everything so messy."

"You need to slow down and explain what the fuck is going on." I paced as fast as I could in socks, wishing to put my boots back on so I could stomp my feet.

"I heard all this from Sheila. It's why she didn't want to give me my mom's last address. Because it's this address. Right where we're both standing." Emerson threw her bag down on the floor. "This is so twisted. My God, I've made a mess of my life," she screamed, tugging wildly at her hair.

I'd never seen her look like this. A mess. Totally out of control.

"Em, this doesn't mean we can't be together. We're not kids, and they're not married anymore. Christ, we didn't even know each other when they were married, I'm guessing. This has no bearing on us," I said, my voice gruff. I was stifling back a combination of anger, tears, and frustration. "My mom would say this is utter nonsense and to think logically."

No matter how much I raged inside, I had to be the strong one here. The one with a clear head. I would fight for the girl in front of me with every last breath of my life.

It was a revelation, and probably not the best time to have it, but so the fuck what. I had it.

"This was her place." Emerson looked up at me, her face red and blotchy, her expression bleak. "In the divorce. I mean, after the divorce, she lived here. Your dad put her up here. He's still desperate to get her clean. I don't know if it will ever happen. She's MIA now, but it doesn't matter. The time I'm sure has passed for me to know her. And for her to know me."

She took a deep breath. "Price, I can't stay here where I'll think of her every day. And I know it's a lot . . . but that's how bad this situation is. I also know this is a bad way to start a relationship. Too many skeletons."

Picking up the duffel, she slung it over her shoulder.

"Wait!" I stilled Em, touching her other shoulder. "None of those skeletons are ours. We are our own people. We grew up and fell for each other despite all those skeletons. Don't you see?"

She shook her head, fresh tears popping out, rolling down her face and leaving black rivers in their wake, but she said nothing.

"Look, I knew this place sucked. I don't care if they were married or whatever. We'll get a different place," I said, making a last-ditch effort. But it didn't mean a damn thing.

Shrugging me off, Emerson looked at me, her eyes glassy and far-off. "Like I said, this isn't about you, Price. Don't make it about you. It's about me. And for God's sake, don't you see the irony? Aren't you going to accuse me of maybe going after you to find my mom?"

"Oh my fucking God." I groaned, so fucking frustrated at Emerson's stubbornness. "I'm not some teeny-bopper or a jilted woman. I didn't think that. I wouldn't think that. We met by accident."

"You don't know that." She brushed by me and headed for the front door.

"I do. Em, you're being unreasonable, in every sense of the word. I'll be right here when you get some sense back in your head."

She didn't reply, only flung open the door and walked toward the elevator.

I chased after her but stopped in the doorway. "You know why? Do you, Emerson? Because I'm falling in love with you."

The elevator dinged as the door opened.

She turned and gave me a sad look. "No, you're not." The doors slid closed, separating me from the only woman I'd ever loved.

CHAPTER
THIRTY-ONE

Price

"Dad!" I yelled into the phone the moment he answered.

"Is everything okay, Price? I know I said I'd be coming to visit, but I ran into a problem. It's not an excuse, just my life."

"No, everything is not okay. My life was fine the way it was before you came riding in with your town car and bags of money."

I paced in front of the floor-to-ceiling windows in *Emerson's mom's apartment*. With her ghost looming and Emerson's absence haunting me, I hadn't been able to sleep for two nights.

"Calm down—"

"No, I can't, *Dad*," I spat out. "I can't calm down because I'm in a city where I don't belong, surrounded by millions of people who don't understand me, and then I meet one who does . . . and you're not going to believe this. She's your wife's daughter." My forehead met the cool glass and I closed my eyes.

"Ex-wife."

"Whatever. Wife, ex-wife. Do you get how awkward shit's become? I'm in love with this woman's daughter, and she's left me because of it. None of this would be happening if you hadn't decided to stroll back into my life like a knight in shining armor. I was fine, and now I'm not. Feel me?"

"I didn't plan for this to happen," my dad said. "I admit when Johnny let me know who you were dating—"

At this point, I'd slumped down on the floor, my back resting on the window. I wanted to smash my head through it. "You knew?"

"Yes, of course," he said, and his voice turned hoarse. "Paula . . . my ex-wife . . . has problems. I don't even know if Emerson knows. Drugs, horrible addiction. The guilt of leaving her daughter behind always tortured her. I found Emerson for Paula years ago and kept tabs on her, and then the girl drove herself to New York on a mission. Lucky kid. She met Sheila. Met you. Considering the odds against it, if I didn't know better, I'd think she planned it."

"Fuck you! Seriously, fuck off. She didn't plan a thing. I don't know the extent of this Paula's problems. But I do know she left her daughter the same way you left me, and she deserves whatever fate she got. Because no one who has a heart does what she did."

"That's why I found you, Price. I couldn't live with myself anymore. It's only cheap talk, I know, but it's all I have. As for my beautiful broken Paula, I guess you got your wish. She died this past weekend of an overdose. Even I couldn't save her."

My dad broke down and wept on the other end of the line, and I couldn't find it in myself to care. Not one single bit.

This would destroy Emerson.

I couldn't be bothered with my relationship with him, or his rescue fantasy, or whatever other shit he had going on. I had more important things to focus on.

"Listen to me." I stood up, fisting my free hand. Thank fuck this conversation wasn't in person, or I would have beaten my own father to a bloody pulp. "You are going to call Emerson and tell her what happened. You're going to tell her every single memory you have about Paula even thinking about her. Make them up, if you don't have them. You're going to tell her how much she regretted leaving her daughter. Again, make this shit up if you have to. You're going to give her closure. Allow Emerson to grieve."

"And what are you going to do?" my dad asked, his voice cracking.

"The fuck? You don't get to make demands of me. You get to do a lot of heavy lifting, and I hope I decide to forgive you for your disappearing act when I was little. For your duplicity now. For moving me into your ex-wife's apartment, knowing I fell for her daughter, and sitting back and watching everything unfold like it's some sort of sick soap opera."

"Do you think you'll ever be able to forgive me?"

"I'll let you know. First things first. I'm going to text you Emerson's number, and you do what I told you to do. I have an apartment to sell . . . and don't you dare say it's not mine to sell. You owe me this and more. And after dealing with all this BS, I have classes to attend."

In all my rage and anger, I realized what I wanted to do with my life and the fucking opportunity that fell in my lap. It would take more of my dad's guilt money, but I couldn't give any fucks.

It was a no-fucks-given kind of day.

Later that night, I lay in bed with what was left of a fifth of bourbon on the bedside table. Sleep was elusive.

Emerson didn't take my call earlier. My head pounded and my heart hurt at not knowing where she was. Finally, I gave in and called her dad. He told me she was at Sheila's place, and he knew what happened.

To say Bend was beating himself up over it was an absolute understatement. I told him it wasn't his fault. Emerson was bound and determined to find her mom. What he didn't know yet was that Paula was dead. I guessed my dad hadn't called Emerson yet.

Grabbing the pillow on Emerson's side of the bed, I breathed in what was left of her scent.

My eyes had just closed, visions of my plan coming to mind, when my phone rang. Jumping up quickly, I hoped it was Emerson.

No such luck. My dad.

"I just hung up with Emerson," he said.

"What took you so long?" I demanded.

"I wanted to make the arrangements first. Paula's parents are both gone now, and I'm all she had."

I didn't give a shit about any of that. "Is Emerson coming to the funeral?" That's what I wanted to know.

"I gave her the details," my dad said.

"I'll be there with you."

At least I knew I'd see Emerson there. There was no way she could stay away.

CHAPTER
THIRTY-TWO

Emerson

At the same time numb and yet torn apart, I stood at my mother's casket in the funeral home, all my emotions bubbling up out of me. I didn't care about the other people in the room, there to mourn her passing. I had a lot to say to this woman who'd birthed me, then left me, and I was going to have my say, no matter what.

"All these years," I said to her pale, still face, my voice broken. "You knew where I was, but you denied me. You . . . you withheld it all from me . . . but why? I need to know, and for God's sake, now you can't tell me. What did I do to deserve this? Be *born*? All I *ever wanted* was someone to care for me more than . . . than themselves. Someone other than Dad. Really, that's the truth."

Leaning closer to her, I said, "I wanted a mom like everyone else." My words were meant to be whisper, but they came out more of a garble.

"I want you to answer me!" A bit of hysteria entered my voice, raw anger bubbling in my throat as I balled my hands into fists. If I didn't keep myself together, I'd grab her poor lifeless body and shake it to death.

Oh, right. She's dead already.

I took a deep breath, trying to control my emotions, but I couldn't help myself.

Panic settled in my gut, slowly rising up my esophagus, but I pushed it back. It slid down my throat into my belly like the sludge at the bottom of a cold cup of coffee.

This damn woman was so pathetic. Laid out in front of me, broken, destroyed by her own demons. She couldn't answer, nor would she ever be able to plead her case or give me the answers I wanted. She couldn't explain what I'd always wanted to know—*needed* to know.

My dad had begged to come with me today, but I'd said no. He didn't deserve to see me mourn a woman who had wronged him so.

It wasn't the body or the casket in front of me causing the hot tears to roll down my cheeks. It was the possibility of what should have been, what could have been mine, and way more. A lifetime of opportunities lost—at least half a lifetime. I would have taken it.

The possibilities had been endless when I'd met Bev and Sheila. At that point, I could have held my mom tight in my arms for the first time in my short eighteen years of life. I'd dreamed of it.

"Emerson, let's go. It's enough pain."

I startled as Bev's hand ran down my back and she spoke in my ear.

These past few days, I couldn't shake Bev if I'd tried. She'd insisted on staying with me, helping me get ready for the funeral, and riding with me in a cab to the funeral home. Sheila had come separately and was sitting in the pews, waiting for the service to start.

I'd been sleeping in Bev's bed with her for the last few nights, feeling so fortunate that my amazing friend had found both forgiveness and compassion for me. My tears flooded my pillow, not only for my mom, but for him. *Price.*

He was gone. It was my doing, but he was gone, nonetheless. I didn't know what I'd been thinking. I couldn't even spell my own name the last few days.

"Em, please, don't do this to yourself. You heard the man . . . her husband," she said softly, careful not to mention Price's father's name. "She regretted her choice, but she didn't have control. She spiraled for most of her life, finding only small pockets of happiness. And you know your dad supports you. He's been enough. It's hard to understand it, but he's been there for you."

I shook my head. Why couldn't I have lived in one of those pockets?

"She doesn't look like the photo your mom showed me," I whispered back, running my hand down my face, swiping away the tears as I studied my mom. They'd plumped her up with whatever they did to dead bodies, painting her face with too much makeup and covering her rail-thin body with long sleeves and pants.

"She hasn't for a long while. Come on, let's go. You saw. There's nothing more to say." Bev pulled on my arm.

Staring at my dead mom, I dug in my heels and stayed put. I didn't let my hand touch the casket, refused to allow myself to say a silent prayer for her, yet tiny wishes for her to be at peace crept into my brain.

The woman inside the box didn't deserve my prayers. But I deserved something.

I'd been denied, and it hurt. Not on a superficial level, but in a way more visceral.

Completely drained, I turned to walk away from the casket, my gaze glued to the carpet, the heat of *his* stare on my back, the singe of *his* touch brushing my hand as I stumbled past, never once stopping.

Price stood tall, his feet grounded as he waited for me to come to him, while the other one—his father—he wept silently in the corner, waiting for my condolences.

I didn't go to either of them.

"I can't stay," I said, leaning into Bev. "I can't do this. I'm sure she was a wonderful person at some point in her life, but I can't hear it."

I couldn't talk anymore. The admission was too much. This was my mom, and now I found myself not able to care. The hurt, the burning pain in my gut, it was too much.

Bev nodded and guided me out the door. She knew there were no words, no platitudes, nothing she could say, and my appreciation for that was unending.

"Emerson!"

Price chased after me into the early autumn day. He didn't get there was nothing he could say. He didn't understand I was barely holding myself together by a thread. After all, he was a dude. He had a primal need to fix this.

I rushed out of the church . . . it was so different from home here. No salt hanging in the air, only mixed with the tears streaming down my face. The world around me was crisp, a light breeze fluttering the dry leaves along the sidewalk. A complete contradiction to the raging feelings punching their way through my bloodstream. I was like a fighter primed on fight night, pumped up and angry, wanting to punch the first face I saw.

"Emerson!"

Bev squeezed my shoulder. "Em, he's desperate to talk with you."

"Emerson!" Price caught up with us. "Please, stop."

I hadn't even realized Bev had let me go, and it was now Price holding me, letting me lean on him.

"I can't! I won't! Stop!" Words flew out of my mouth. I didn't even know what I wanted him to stop. I wanted the whole goddamn world to stop. Without a thought, my fist formed, and I was punching his bicep and his chest. "Move! You have to let me be!"

"No!" He stood unflinching in front of me, taking a beating not meant for him. "Em, hurt me. Do what you need to."

That was Price. Selfless, compassionate, the opposite of my mom. He was like my dad, the only constant I'd ever known.

Unable to stop myself, I hit him once more and then fell back on my butt, landing in a pile of leaves.

Price dropped down next to me and cradled me like a baby. "Listen, I know you're hurting, but please don't push me away. I'm here for you. Not only Bev. I'm. Here. Too."

At the sound of her name, I looked up to find Bev. "Where is she?" Hysteria crept up my throat. "She's a good friend. Did you make her go? Did she leave?"

"She is a great friend," he said softly, swiping my hair behind my ear. "She's more than a good friend. But she saw I'm with you, and she went in to sit with her mom. She knows I can take care of you . . . that I want to take care of you."

"Oh. Sheila must be devastated too. She couldn't do a thing . . . to help my mom. She must be dying over it on the inside. More than the cancer already is—"

My words cut off when Price placed his lips on mine. It wasn't a lustful kiss. It was consoling, comforting.

"Shhh," he whispered, our mouths no longer fused, but still close enough to tickle each other. "I know this is bad timing, but I have to tell you this. I love you, Emerson. We didn't expect it to happen or to find it when we ran into each other that first time, but we did. I know you care for me more than I ever dreamed you could, and my feelings for you run two-, three-fold yours. I promise you that."

"What?"

My head jerked back, and I looked into Price's eyes. His hair was a mess, and his suit was getting wrinkled and dirty as he knelt with me.

"I love you. And none of this means anything. Not your mom or my dad, or their shit. Of course, your pain . . . it means everything. And I'm here for you. Come back with me. We can stay at a hotel with Tuck. He misses you. I can't breathe without you."

"That apartment. I never want to go back there."

"I don't either," he said softly into my neck. "We can go to the hotel on the next block. Don't be mad, but your dad is there. I had him come up. He called me a little while after you walked out, afraid that you might run. He loves you. I love you. We want you to understand you're loved."

"I don't want him to see me like this."

"He doesn't care. He loves you so much. He's giving you space, even though he doesn't want to. But he knows you're grieving, and he's okay with that."

Exhaustion overwhelmed me, and I let my forehead rest on his shoulder.

A few hours later, I woke up in a strange bed, in an unfamiliar room, wearing nothing but my bra and panties. Strung out didn't begin to describe how I felt.

Tired, lost, cold . . . A shiver ran through me, and my whole body shook.

"Hey."

A voice came from the side of the room, and I turned. Price sat on a couch in what was obviously a hotel suite.

"Let me turn the heat up. You're cold," he said quietly. He stood with purpose and moved to the thermostat.

"When did I fall asleep?" I tried to sit up in the bed, but only fell back into the stack of down pillows.

"In the car. Johnny helped me get you up here, but only I took your clothes off."

He didn't wink or smirk. The words were matter-of-fact, as if I would think he would allow another man to see me nearly naked.

CHAPTER
THIRTY-THREE

Price

I met the ass in the lobby. He'd begged me to do so.

Emerson was still wrung out and sitting with her dad—there was no reason to force my dad on her at the moment.

"Price," he said in greeting, pulling me in for a hug.

It was the first moment of affection we'd ever shared. I didn't know how it made me feel, but this wasn't the time for my feelings. Stepping back, I cleared my throat. We stood there, two men squaring off in the lobby of this uppity hotel.

"Let's sit down for a minute," he said.

I nodded, and we found two highbacked, uncomfortable-as-shit chairs.

"I didn't mean for any of this to happen." My dad choked on his words, his own pain visible in the dark circles under his eyes. "I thought Paula was out of the woods. For a while, she was doing better. She didn't want me back in her life, especially after I'd gone and found you. It was too painful. She hadn't been able to do the same, and on some level, she couldn't stand herself for that."

Running my hand through my greasy hair, I realized it had been close to two days since I'd showered. It didn't matter; I'd been busy doing what I had to.

"These are things I don't need to hear," I said abruptly to my dad.

"Yes, I know, but I'm guessing you're not going to let me get face-to-face with Emerson for some time, so I thought you could relay the message. Please?"

I nodded, and he went on.

"This is my doing. I don't want you to blame yourself, but when I reconnected with you . . . Paula lost it. She couldn't stop dwelling in the woulda, coulda, shoulda if she'd connected with her daughter. You have to know the background . . . for the longest time, we were both a mess. We'd both lost the most precious thing ever—our kids—thanks to our own doing. But together, we were whole."

He pulled in a deep breath, blinking hard. "Then we unraveled, divorced, for no reason other than we should've never fallen for each other—or anyone, for that matter. My reuniting with you messed with Paula, and she started really heavy using again, whatever she could get her hands on. She'd already been dabbling again. She'd left the apartment a few months before I went to get you . . . had run off with a young guy for a bit, and then she floundered."

Tears welled in my dad's eyes. "Anyway, now she's gone for good. It's all on me. I failed her."

I should have felt something at seeing his pain, but I couldn't dredge up anything. "Listen, it sounds like she was a really damaged person. None of this is your fault. I don't know what to say about us, but in terms of Paula, you did all you could." It was about all that I could offer up.

His hand came to rest on top of mine, and even I didn't have the heart to move it. "I need this. Us. Whatever little or more it can be. I'm all alone, Price. I know I've not done a single thing right, but I'm going to try. For you, and for Emerson . . . in memory of Paula."

I couldn't make myself agree. Not now. When it came to Emerson, there had been too many empty promises.

"Okay," I said. "Look, I need to get back up to Emerson. She's my main priority right now, and I can't even think about anything else . . . not now. Let's talk more later. Leave it open?"

I stood, and he followed suit.

"Please call me," he said, his voice weak.

I nodded and walked toward the elevator.

Outside the hotel room door, I stilled my hand. I wanted to barge in, grab Emerson, and take her home to the farm, just leave this shithole city behind. But I couldn't rush her—I knew better than that. Plus, I didn't even know if she wanted to move to the farm.

Leaning my head against the wall, I squeezed my eyes shut, knowing I'd stay or do whatever she wanted. Go to the beach, stay here, move home . . . it made no difference, as long as we were together. Pulling in a deep breath, I pulled out my keycard.

"I'm back," I said softly, opening the door.

"Hey," she said to me from the couch.

"Hey, you. Where's your dad?"

"Shower. We had a good cry, and then I needed a break from him."

I sat next to her, gathered all her limbs in my arms, and held her tight—probably too tight. "He loves you."

"It was enough," she said. "It always was. I don't know what I was looking for in all this. He should've always been enough."

"He was. But you can't blame yourself for wanting to meet your mom."

Emerson nodded into my shoulder. "I did. I really did. I'm sorry she had to die . . . because now my questions will never be answered. I know that's selfish, but it's the truth. I just wanted to know why."

"It's not selfish. You're just a girl looking for answers. No one would blame you."

She held on to me as if I held all the answers. It made me feel like I had the world in the palms of my working-guy's hands.

"I love you," I told her. "Your dad loves you. My mom is going to love you. You're building your own family, Em. Bev. Sheila. Me. My mom and Bruce—you have to meet them."

"Yeah, I know. I do. But . . . but are you sure?" Emerson hesitated, stammering over her words. "You're okay with us being together? And your dad understands? This feels so complicated."

Pulling back, making a little space between us, I pushed her hair aside. "It's not complicated. We had nothing to do with them. It's only us right now. I don't want that to be what you're worried about. My dad is fine, but honestly? I wouldn't care if he wasn't. He's the last thing I'm thinking about. You're first, if you couldn't tell."

"Don't say that about your dad, 'kay? I'm sorry, I don't mean to boss you. I'm so out of it. I just don't want to feel like I'm a problem in your relationship . . . and I love you too," she whispered.

"You're it for me," I told her. "Enough for me. For always. My future was set. I was going to be a farmer, and now I don't know what I'm going to do. As long as you're with me, that's all that matters."

"Farmer Price." She gave me a small smile, the first I'd seen from her in what seemed like forever. "With his boots," she teased me.

"You need some boots, and you'll see what I mean."

"Uh-huh." She leaned in and rubbed her nose along mine.

We didn't talk anymore. Instead, we kissed, our lips meeting on their own accord. We stayed like that for a long while, until Bend cleared his throat and faked a cough.

"Oh, Dad!" Emerson jumped up.

"It's fine, baby. I was just going to say that I'm going to meet up with that Sheila woman. I guess she had some things she always wanted to tell me from when I knew your mom."

"Oh. Okay. You know her daughter, Bev, is my good friend now."

He stood tall in his jeans and ragged polo shirt, ancient New Balance joggers on his feet, looking completely out of place in the Big Apple. Like I did.

Oh well, fuck it. We belonged here as much as anyone else. Even if we thought it was the craziest place.

"Don't worry," Bend said. "I know. I'm not going to do anything to mess it up for you with Bev."

"Love you, Dad." Emerson stood up to hug her dad.

"I know. But I love you more," he said, and then slipped out of the hotel room.

"Sheila? That's crazy," Emerson said to me, sitting back on my lap.

"She asked me for your dad's number. I didn't think she'd connect with him so soon, but maybe because it's fresh, she wants to rip the Band-Aid off quickly."

"I don't know. It's a little crazy, but no crazier than any of this."

Emerson leaned her head on my shoulder, and her stomach growled. "Sorry," she said with a laugh.

I squeezed her hand. "Come on. Let's shower and go eat."

We took a little longer in the shower and ended up ordering room service, which was fine with me.

CHAPTER
THIRTY-FOUR

Emerson

"We can't stay in this hotel forever. It's crazy. Plus, I miss your pancakes," I told Price over another room service breakfast. I'd lost count of how many we'd had. Thirteen? Fourteen?

"I'm working on it. I swear. Today, after I go to class, Johnny's gonna shuttle me around . . . Christ. Do you know how insane this all is?" He laughed while saying it, but still.

"I can tell the ridiculousness is getting to you. I know your dad's footing the bill. I also know the apartment sold in minutes, so we can buy anything. Sorry, not we. *You.* You can buy anything."

He tugged on a strand of my hair, leaning in and placing his lips on my forehead. "We, ours, all of it. Shhh. Don't forget Paula was your mom, and it was her place."

"Listen here, buddy. You can't use Paula to your convenience."

In the last week, I'd decided I needed some emotional distance from the whole situation and had started to refer to my mom as Paula. She was a person I'd never know. Before my dad left, I reconciled myself to that fact. My dad had always been there and would continue to be. It was more than I could ask of—

"Get out of the clouds, Em. If I see something cool, I'm going to put in an offer tonight. Is that okay? Or do you want to ask Bev for some more time off?"

"No, you pick. Honestly. Make sure it's good for Tuck."

Momentarily distracted by Price shirtless, in nothing but navy pajama pants, I drank him in. For a second, I bit my tongue, making sure this was real.

"You happy to be back at the bakery?"

"Yes," I said with confidence. "I really am. Sheila decided not to come back full-time, which gives me more hours and responsibility. I love it."

"Good, and the bar? You going to miss it?"

"Don't start. You and my dad forced the issue. I have to do something else."

On another kiss, he said, so close our lips were touching, "Well, I have some ideas on that."

"Oh yeah, does it involve your cooking? I'm so sick of this stuck-up stuff."

"In fact, it does," he said, sitting back in the chair.

"Care to share?"

"Yeah, after I go to class and then find us a place to live. How 'bout we ditch these ritzy digs for the farm this weekend? My mom is crawling out of her skin wanting to meet you. She even said she'd make an apple pie."

"Ha, funny. Sounds great, though. But is she okay with your dad and what happened with my mom? Are you sure she's cool?"

"Yes. Stop."

Price stood and pulled me up, fully kissing me, tongue and all, and smacked my butt before saying, "Wish me luck. I have a test this morning."

"Luck," I said, planting a kiss on his cheek.

He winked and was out the hotel door.

I hit the shower, excited to get to the bakery and try my hand at a new crème brûlée recipe with a hint of lemon. If it went well, we could sell it in individual ramekins.

My mind wandered as I lathered my body. This wasn't at all what I thought would happen when I ran away from home, but it was turning out not half bad.

We drove up to Pennsylvania Saturday morning. Tuck got hair all over the expensive car, but Price was completely unconcerned with it.

"After we get a new place to live," he said, "I'm getting rid of the Tesla. We don't even need it. I'll give my dad the money back, but he'll push it back on me. Guilt money."

"Maybe it's not. Maybe he genuinely wants to help you in the only way he can. I mean . . . I never heard her side of the story, but it sounds like he tried to help Paula."

Price nodded. "Then we'll get a truck."

I didn't argue anymore. I knew better than anyone else that he'd have to come to terms with the situation on his own.

He had found a loft for us, and of course, refused to put in an offer until I saw it this morning before we left town. It was light and open, and located in a neighborhood way more suited for us. It would be good—the right choice, I hoped.

Price turned the Tesla off the highway and onto a long driveway, which ended at the coolest (and first) farmhouse I'd ever seen. Before we were even fully out of the car, an older couple came down the steps to meet us.

"Hi, Emerson, welcome! I'm Sarah."

Price's mom let out a squeal and pulled me in for a gigantic bear hug. I was lost in a sea of her limbs, my frame tiny next to her taller one, and I was lost in a jumble of emotions.

The words clogged in my throat, and I could barely get out, "Me too. It's so nice to be here."

"Mom, let Em breathe." Price stole me back into his embrace, and I settled in the circle of his arm—willingly and happily.

"Bruce," the tall man next to Sarah said, extending his hand.

"So great to meet you," I told him.

"Come in." Sarah herded us toward the house, grinning from ear to ear.

"Forgive my wife. I don't know if she's more excited to see the light of her life, her son, or meet you."

I tried to smile but felt a frown form. *I'll never have a mother excited to see me.*

"I'm so sorry," Bruce said, catching my expression. "That was insensitive. I should say I'm sorry about your loss. Your mom."

Price murmured, "Shit."

When I caught him shaking his head, I squeezed his hand. Taking a deep breath, I collected myself.

"No, don't feel that way. You can't protect me from the world," I said, side-eyeing Price as we stepped inside the house.

With a slow glance, I took in all that was around me. Family pictures, heirlooms, flannel blankets on the couch . . . it was a real honest-to-goodness home.

"You know what? I just met you, but I'm going to tell you what I know. I just walked in here, and it's a home. A real home, made by a mom who loves Price. But I had a similar home, only made by a dad. He loved me more than anything, and he did better than his best."

Gathering me back in his embrace, Price kissed the top of my head and held me tight. "Let's not stand in the doorway," he said, breaking the seriousness.

"I cooked!" Sarah ran off toward what I assumed was the kitchen.

"And I made dessert. It's in the back so Tuck wouldn't get it," I said, motioning toward the car.

"Let's get those jackets off and settle in, yeah? Price, go get the food," Bruce said, holding a hand out for my jacket. Price opened the door, and an eager Tuck followed him out to the car.

Bruce showed me the way to the kitchen, and I gasped.

"This place is so perfect. It's awesome."

"I love it. We redid it a few years ago," Sarah told me. "Price helped with some of the work. He's pretty handy. I guess in the big city, though, that doesn't matter."

"Mom," Price said in a warning voice as he walked back in, holding my tray of ramekins.

"I know, honey. I didn't mean anything. You're doing big things there, and that's what I always wanted for you."

She smiled at her son. Wearing a crisp white blouse and an apron, a few threads of gray at her temples, Sarah was every bit a proud momma.

"This is what I wanted to talk to you about," Price said. "I think I want to open a restaurant. Sorry to blurt it out. It's a lot of seriousness in the first few minutes of this visit. But I'm not sure I'm coming back here."

The pace of this conversation was like a Ping-Pong game. Way too fast for me, but I went with it.

"In New York?" Bruce asked, opening a beer.

"Yep, or maybe in the beach town where Emerson grew up, if she changes her mind. I only sprang this on her late last night. Are you upset?"

"No, son." Bruce walked around and threw his arm around Price's shoulders.

"Never," Sarah said. "We always wanted you to do whatever makes you happy. But the restaurant business is tough . . . and do you know anything about it?"

"I've been doing a lot of research on it in my classes. I think my idea is unique enough, and I bring the right stuff to the table. I want to build something with a piece of home. Fresh homegrown ingredients in the city, *think rooftops instead of water towers* is my motto. I've been outlining it in my head, and I tossed the idea around with one of my professors."

"What about your degree?" Sarah asked, and I hoped she didn't ask me. I liked baking and working, and I hoped to play a part in the restaurant without actually having to go to college to do it. I'd spent a good part of the night thinking about it.

"I'm still going to get it," Price said. "But I have these funds available to me, and I know what I want to do with them."

"If you're thinking it, I know it's a solid plan," Bruce said, encouraging him.

Now I was grinning, cheesing like the happy, proud girlfriend. Why? Because Price's idea was stellar.

"Well, let's eat, and you can tell me if it's any good," Sarah teased.

We sat down around their big farm table, and I'd never laughed or smiled as much as I did in that one hour. We finished with Sarah's apple pie and my caramel crème brûlées.

"I don't know about the restaurant food, but the desserts are going to be fabulous," Bruce said as he cleared the table.

"I feel exactly the same," Price said with a wink at me, and stood up to help Bruce.

CHAPTER
THIRTY-FIVE

Price

"Come on," I said, helping Emerson up to the top of the water tower.

We sat on the ledge in the darkness, nothing but stars above us. Our legs dangled in the air, her much smaller pair of shitkickers knocking with mine. With her head on my shoulder, it was a perfect moment.

"It's too quiet for me," I admitted.

"Ha, is that so?"

"I need to hear an ambulance or a police siren."

"Thanks for bringing me," she said, changing the subject.

"Anytime. We can come anytime. My mom would love it. And I do like being here."

I pulled Emerson closer and breathed her in. I used to love the morning dew . . . that smell was how I knew I was home. Now I loved the smell of this girl.

"You're my home now," I said into the night.

"Do you think it's too soon?"

"I don't. I hate to believe in crazy hoodoo-voodoo, but when we're sitting here, looking at the stars, I have to believe there's a greater plan. And we met as part of that plan. I was wandering through life, content with how I grew up, and then thrown into this new place, lost for the first time, looking for direction. You were also wandering, and looking for love. And we both found what we needed in each other."

"I did find love. You. Bev. Sheila. I wanted the love of my mom, but maybe what I found is better, or what I was supposed to find."

"I think so. I know so," I told her, and then guided her mouth toward mine.

We kissed on top of the water tower, and the place held new meaning for me.

Emerson pulled away and glanced over the edge. "We're going to fall off of here."

"Ha, come on." I guided her back safely to the ground and took her hand in mine. "Where you grew up, it's the sand dunes. Here, it's the back of a truck."

"Oh, yes." She skipped a step, getting my meaning.

"You sure?" I stilled in the darkness on the way back to the truck.

"I'm sure."

When we made it back to the spot in the field where I'd parked, I opened a blanket and set some music on my phone instead of the dash—I was mostly a New Yorker now.

We lay facing each other for a while, kissing, running our hands down each other's backs. Then Emerson's hand was under my shirt, and she pinched my nipple. I moaned, and it was all over. My shirt came off, and so did hers.

I pulled a second blanket over us and unhooked her bra. My mouth traveled the length of her neck, making its way toward her cleavage. In no rush, I took my time there, listening to Em's soft whimpers.

When she begged, "Please," I slid down and took her jeans, panties, and boots with me. Nestling between her thighs, I made her go wilder until she declared she couldn't take it anymore.

Shucking off my own boots and jeans in a pile at our feet, I slid back in between us. With no barriers, I made love to Emerson, and decided it didn't matter where I lived or what I did.

I never had to wander anymore—except home to her.

EPILOGUE

Emerson

Three years later

It was Friday, the last one in May, and the rain had finally stopped long enough for us to bolt from the parking lot into the assembly hall for Price's graduation. The ceremony was a formality at this point, but I'd told him he had to go. I needed a picture of him in his cap and gown (*duh*), despite his current success.

His dad sent congratulations via text, and of course, I had to make Price text back *thanks* in return. Their relationship remained strained, but I hoped it would improve. I think Price secretly wanted it to as well, but pride kept him from admitting it. That, and respect for his mom held him back. He didn't want to betray her, even though she'd said he wasn't doing that a million and one times.

They'd never be super close. But his father truly had no one, and I believed somewhere deep down, Price cared for him. Together, they could support each other in some capacity. I had a feeling it would happen sooner rather than later . . . after I spoke with Price this evening.

As for now, his mom and stepdad, along with my dad, weren't coming today, but planned their trip to New York City the following day for a celebratory lunch at Emmy B's. They'd all been a few times already, and had been amazed by the majestic big city and the small slice of rural paradise Price had built there.

Sheila and Bev were coming tomorrow too. That was no surprise anymore. My dad and Sheila had an unnamed thing going on now that she was in remission. Bev and I didn't get involved in the dynamics of it, other than saying we were sisters now. I'd certainly gone from having just a dad to having a big family . . . pretty quickly.

As for Emmy B's, the restaurant might have taken the West Village by surprise with its rooftop garden and farm-to-table cuisine, but it was no shock to me. Combining his two loves, Price built the place from the ground up. I expected nothing less from him. I always smiled when he talked about his inspiration for it: combining me and farm life.

The seating around the rooftop garden looked out from its heavy foliage onto the concrete streets of New York. With lights strung above and tea lights around the edge of the roof, it was recently voted the most romantic spot in New York. Price was noted as bringing his love of everything small-town Pennsylvania to the big city. Pleasing the palates of the Big Apple was no easy task.

"Look what it says here, Em."

Price knocked me out of my thoughts as we walked into the assembly hall. Of course, he'd been walking and reading on his phone. After all, he was a New Yorker now, but I wasn't going to be the one to tell him that. I let him think he was still only part hipster.

"*Completing the meal at Emmy B's,*" he read out loud, "*were the in-house dessert creations of Bev Brantley and Emerson Bender. Bender, the namesake for Emmy B's—and owner Price Barnes's better half—has been with the restaurant since its inception. After eating her Caramel-Infused Apple Blondie smothered in homemade caramel drizzle and topped with fresh whipped cream and cherries,*

I'm in agreement—she is definitely the better half. Bender and Brantley met at the Lucky Artist Bakery, which they now co-own and run with the help of Seany Michaels, known to the New York food scene for his creations at the Coffee Bar.

"Notably, Brantley dances on the side, and she recently starred in an off-Broadway show.

"Now, it's a well-known fact that Brantley and Bender are opening the Milk and Cookies Bar in the spot two doors down from Emmy B's. I can't say I'm not excited . . . the Boyfriend Cookie Sundae at Emmy B's is triple sin in a dish."

"Okay, stop." I ran my hand down Price's arm and snatched his phone. "It's your day."

"Did you hear what they said in the *Times*?"

"Yes, I saw it this morning."

I'd gone to culinary school for some baking courses and then decided to just wing it. My dad and Price had both told me not to close any doors, that maybe I'd return to school one day.

But I'm not going to lie. I loved what I did on a daily basis, and I had no desire to go back to school. At the restaurant and the Milk and Cookies Bar was where I was going to spend most of my time. The dessert bar would be my first baby, and I was in full-on nesting mode when it came to the grand opening.

Seany was planning to buy the bakery from us and expand it into more of a funky luncheonette. Also, I'd turned twenty-two a month ago, and I didn't think going back to school was in me. Price was a special breed who could go as a returning adult. It must be that farm-boy patience. Me, I was too impatient when it came to everything.

Maybe that was something I got from Paula. I'd never know. I did know my dad loved me enough for two parents, even when I'd tried to find my mom. I'd been the one looking, and she'd been hiding. There was nothing else I could do for her or her situation, and I'd finally resigned myself to accepting that it had nothing to do with me. She had been in a bad way, and my heart always dipped when I thought about how troubled she must have been.

"Now, go," I told Price. "Go line up or sit down or whatever until they call your name."

I didn't have time to dwell on things. It was go time for Price. My true love.
I might have been young, too young, when we met, but it didn't matter. When
your heart is wandering and looking for love and you find it, you grab it and
hold on to it.

After Price became a college graduate at the age of twenty-six, we went to
Emmy B's for a celebratory drink. Of course, while he was there, he checked
on every little detail. Thankfully, he didn't notice the exchange between the
bartender, Chuck, and me . . . it was nothing illicit, and he'd know soon enough.

Once the restaurant closed for the night, we went home to the place Price
found for us after he sold his apartment. Now we lived on the top floor of a loft
in the Meatpacking District with a huge rooftop balcony, and plenty of room
for Tuck to run around. It was more us, and we loved it there.

The two of us lay in bed, twisted in the sheets, kissing like we did every
night, Price running his hand down my back.

"I love you," he said into my back, his breath tickling the nape of my neck.
"Turn around for a sec."

I rolled around in his arms, and he reached behind him, into the nightstand
drawer.

"What are you doing?" I asked as he rummaged in the drawer. "A condom?
We don't need it."

"You and your one-track mind. Sex, sex, sex." He kissed my forehead and
pulled back. When he raised his hand, something sparkly hung off his pinky.
"Emerson Paige Bender, will you marry me?"

Typical Price. He didn't wait for the "perfect" time or plan something
extravagant. He knew what he wanted, and he went for it.

"Wow." I had no words, hardly able to believe this was happening now. *Now, of all times.*

"That ring," I said, taking in the single gorgeous solitaire on a slender platinum band. It was perfect—huge—but the simple design was all me.

"Well?" Price took the ring and slipped it onto my finger.

"Yes! Of course. Ring or not, I planned to spend the rest of my life with you."

"Is that so?"

"Pretty much. I guess it's a good time to tell you something else."

"What? Your name isn't really Emerson? You're a spy?"

"Ha! I'm not exactly sure how to say this, so I'm just gonna come out with it. We're going to have a baby."

"What?" He shot up in bed, his naked, muscular chest stealing my gaze like it always did.

"A baby. Me. You. In November. Remember when I had the ear infection? We didn't pay attention to the warning about the antibiotic possibly messing with the pill, and then our rendezvous in the storage closet in the Milk and Cookies Bar?"

"Oh, I remember," he said, smirking. "But you had a cocktail a few hours ago. You've been drinking vodka all month."

I shook my head. "Soda and cran. Chuck's been in on the plan, and that's all he serves me. Makes it look real."

"You little devil. What were you waiting for?" He pulled me close for a deep kiss.

"For you to graduate, be everything I knew you could be. I was going to tell everyone tomorrow after lunch. I wanted today to be all about you. But now we're engaged, and everyone will think you proposed because of the bun in the oven."

"Never. We both have been holding in a secret. Tomorrow was going to be a surprise engagement party. Chuck's in on it too, the shit. He's been playing both sides of this operation."

I pouted out my bottom lip. "I wanted you to have a party all about you."

"Em, nothing could make me happier. A baby, a wife. Now, be quiet and go back to your sexy thoughts."

P r i c e
Seven months later

"Shhh," I whispered to the little bundle in my arms. "Let Mommy sleep, deal?" I bargained with my three-week-old daughter as if I wouldn't give her anything and everything she wanted.

Rebecca Barnes came into the world a week early on a Thursday at two o'clock in the morning, and she'd been making herself known since the minute she arrived. I'd banked on her being a spitfire like her mom, and I wasn't wrong. With thick jet-black hair and big blue eyes—we hoped they didn't change—and olive skin from me, she was already a beauty queen.

"We may need a Rottweiler too," I told an extremely tired Tuck, who sat guard at my feet.

His routine had been slightly upset after the baby's birth, but Tuck didn't care. With doting eyes, he watched Becca. At least he had a small yard to run around in now that we lived in a brownstone over in Brooklyn. The loft was fun, but not fit for a family.

"Hey."

Emerson appeared in the doorway, looking sleepy but gorgeous in wrinkled pajamas, buttons askew, her hair a mess, and slippers on her feet.

"Is she hungry?" she asked, stretching her neck from side to side.

"Could be, but she's quiet now in my arms. Let her be."

"You have that effect on girls."

She came close and took a now wide-eyed Becca from my arms, and I immediately stood, making room for her in the rocker.

Of course, Tuck sat up and rested his chin on Em's knee while she fed our daughter. According to him, no one—not even me—was allowed to disturb Mom and baby during mealtime.

I leaned against the nursery wall, watching my beautiful wife, thinking about how I was a lucky dude.

Catching the small painting on the far wall of three pairs of shitkickers— large, medium, and small, our names underneath a pair painted for each of us—I couldn't help but smile. You could take the farm boy out of the farm and place him in the big city, where he could fall in love, build an empire, and move to Brooklyn, but you could never make him give up his shitkickers.

Thankfully, I fell for a girl who didn't make me.

ACKNOWLEDGMENTS

Saying thanks is hard. I never know where to start and when to stop.

This book makes it an even dozen, and I already have another one mostly baked . . . and I have the same team since day one.

Thank you to my editor, Pam Berehulke, for her never-ending patience and not-so-gentle red pen. The jelly to my sun butter, one can't go without the other. Truly!

Much appreciation and admiration for Sarah Hansen on blowing me away with another stellar cover.

To Virginia Carey, you've had a part in every single damn book . . . and you were the first person I met in the book world!

Christy and Fab, we've been by one another's virtual side since day one. We may be scattered at far ends of the world, but when we need one another, we are there. #soapythighs

Jenn Watson, there's not enough space. Same goes for you—Sarah, Brooke, and the rest of the Social Butterfly gang. Who else would deal with my robo-emailing and lunatic questions 24/7? Oh, and release my damn book!

The amazing team at E.M. Tippetts, you have made every one of my books WORK! And look good!

To all the bloggers . . . I get it. You work hard. AND it doesn't go unnoticed. Thanks for making the book world go round.

For my ELECTRIC READERS . . . yeah, you. You're the freaking best, and don't forget it.

And to all the readers in the wide-wide-world, thank you.

xo
Rachel

ABOUT THE AUTHOR

Rachel Blaufeld is a bestselling author of Romantic Suspense, New Adult, Coming-of-Age Romance, and Sports Romance. A recent poll of her readers described her as *insightful, generous, articulate,* and *spunky.* Originally a social worker, Rachel creates broken yet redeeming characters. She's been known to turn up the angst like cranking up the heat in the dead of winter.

A devout coffee drinker and doughnut eater, Rachel spends way too many hours in local coffee shops, downing the aforementioned goodies while she plots her ideas. Her tales may all come with a side of angst and naughtiness, but end as lusciously as her treats.

As a side note, Blaufeld, also a long-time blogger and an advocate of woman-run anything, is fearless about sharing her opinion. To her, work/life/family balance is an urban legend, but she does her best.

Rachel has also blogged for *The Huffington Post, Modern Mom,* and *USA TODAY,* where she shared conversations at "In Bed with a Romance Author" and reading recommendations at "Happy Ever After."

Rachel lives around the corner from her childhood home in Pennsylvania with her family and two beagles. Her obsessions include running, coffee, basketball, icing-filled doughnuts, antiheroes, and mighty fine epilogues.

When she isn't writing, she can be found courtside, tweeting about hoops as her son plays, or walking around the house wearing earplugs while her other son, the drummer, bangs away.

To connect with Rachel, she's most active in her private reading group, *The Electric Readers,* where she shares insider information and intimate conversation with her readers:

Tunnel VIPs

As well as:

www.rachelblaufeld.com
Twitter
Facebook
Newsletter

If you liked this book, feel free to leave a review where you bought it or on Goodreads. Send me an e-mail when you do, and I will thank you personally!

www.ingramcontent.com/pod-product-compliance
Lightning Source LLC
Chambersburg PA
CBHW070108260626
47160CB00004B/1374